FIXING THIS BROKEN THING...

The American Criminal Justice System

James B Bolen, Ph.D.

PAGE PUBLISHING, INC.
New York, NY

First originally published by Page Publishing, Inc. 2018

ISBN 978-1-64138-694-4 (Paperback)
ISBN 978-1-64138-695-1 (Digital)

Printed in the United States of America

INTRODUCTION

How much confidence do you have in this Criminal Justice System? What do you expect of the court system? Are you confident that your local government is using the most effective means available to recruit and train your police force? What do you believe is the most accurate measure of your Criminal Justice System? Does the current Criminal Code (laws) adequately address issues of crime and disorder in our communities? When examining our Criminal Justice System, one can find fault with each aspect of this system. I would be remiss if I did not initially state that this book will not provide, suggest or illustrate the "magic pill" which will solve all the problems with our Criminal Justice System. However, it does address a variety of topics, and it does provide methodology to address each concern raised.

Justice...when we utilize the services of our Criminal Justice System, it is reasonable to expect that justice shall prevail. Justice can be fairly defined as conformity to moral righteousness: attainment of what is fair and equitable. We are a nation of laws, and the law should ensure that justice prevails. However, far too often, justice is not realized during the utilization of our Criminal Justice System. "Good" does not always overcome "evil." "Right" does not vanquish "wrong." The injured do not always attain justice. I recognize that this system was developed by human beings, and we are imperfect. Hence, anything we develop cannot be perfect. However, after working in this Criminal Justice System academically and professionally for more than twenty years, I am compelled to offer this book. The amount of injustice that exists in our Criminal Justice System is simply intolerable. Far too often, the injured seek to redress their grievances by utilizing this system and are left sorely disappointed. There is an ever-growing frustration with this Criminal Justice System that could lead our society devolving into anomie. Gloom and doom prophecies can easily be characterized as the ravings of an irrational and overly dramatic mad person. We've all heard the "we're in the last days" declarations. But there is a saturation point beyond which the masses will not allow their frustrations to exceed. Based upon my studies of this system, working in it and observing how it operates, I have come to conclude this system is in desperate need of a make-over. Our Criminal Justice System cannot continue to operate this inefficiently.

During the course of this book, I am going to support my argument by sharing incidents I've experienced professionally, statistics from various sources and recounting various newsworthy events. Other professionals and/or academics in this field will seek to counter my arguments with various facts and figures. A wise man once told me, "There are lies, damned lies and statistics." Donald Riddle, chancellor emeritus, University of Illinois Chicago Circle Campus. There are statistics to illustrate that the violent crime rate is in decline. Statistics that indicate how many offenders have been arrested and convicted. There are more people in American prisons than any other prison system on this planet. But how safe do you feel? I encourage you to think about the circumstances in which you live.

While working on my master's degree, I traveled to Vienna, Austria with fellow Criminal Justice students to conduct a comparative analysis of the two justice systems. I observed that even though Vienna was a fairly large metropolis, there were some streets that did not have the benefit of artificial streetlights. Hence, I conducted a VERY nonscientific experiment. I walked some of those nonlit streets after dark to observe the citizenry. What I observed was people traveling about with little if any concern. Women traveled alone, did not cross the street as myself or other men approached. They did not clutch their purses or look over their shoulders as they walked past strangers. I could detect absolutely no tension in the air, and each person I observed seemed to be as comfortable as if the sun was out and brightly shining. Austria has very strict gun laws, so I can't attribute their sense of comfort to the fact that they were armed. I concede that I spent only a brief time there, but I just marveled at what I observed. I was shocked to learn that while there was a police presence on the streets, the police stations were closed. At that time, I was a Chicago police officer, and I just could not imagine any circumstance where closing the police stations would be prudent. The thought of closing police stations at night in a major metropolis was as foreign to me as the Chinese alphabet. I grew up on the south side of Chicago. I was a Chicago police officer. In my mind, there had to be something radically different about this society.

There are those in our society that believe arming our citizenry will make our nation safer. The National Rifle Association (NRA) purports itself as THE defender of our Second Amendment right to keep and bear arms. I have come to question the sincerity of that organization. I question its actual goal. Since 2007, our Congress has been working to pass legislation that would not allow persons on the federal "no-fly list" the right to purchase firearms. The people on that list are suspected terrorists or in the very least suspected to terrorist sympathizers. Our intelligence agencies have determined that allowing them to board aircraft would risk the safety and security of the fellow passengers and unsuspecting citizens on the ground. However, the NRA has worked diligently to defeat this legislation at every turn. This is offensively stupid. Any person that is too dangerous to board an aircraft is most assuredly too dangerous to own or possess a firearm. And any person that has been unjustly or errantly placed upon the federal "no-fly list" can dispute such and have that rectified. The NRA has consistently fought any effort to restrict the sale of armor-piercing ammunition to the general public (cop killers). This ammunition easily penetrates the bullet-resistant vests worn by law enforcement professionals. There is no defendable reason that the general public need be equipped with ammunition that pierces the bullet-resistant vests worn by police officers. I reflected upon my own experience after purchasing a firearm and looked at NRA publications that I received. Most of the content of these publications were sales ads for various firearms manufacturers. It appears to me that the primary objective of the NRA is to protect the profit margin of the gun industry. Their objective appears to be to work as lobbyists for gun manufacturers and defeat any causes of action that would decrease the sales of firearms regardless of the consequences. NRA officials represent themselves as loyal Americans. I must question their sincerity to the overall good of our nation when they work against legislation that clearly is crafted to protect Americans from groups that have sworn to hurt us. Furthermore, the NRA must accept the fact that protecting the citizens of this nation is appreciably more important than the profit margin of the gun industry.

I ask that you read this book with an open mind. There are parts of this book that will challenge your ability to maintain an open mind. This book is intended to motivate you to reconsider much of what you believe you know about our Criminal Justice System. The target audience is "you the people" of this great nation as I am convinced the change necessary to fix this broken thing will not be initiated by our elected officials. In fact, this book illustrates that many of our elected officials are disingenuous in their collective proclamation of concern for our safety. Our Criminal Justice System will be fixed when the people of our nation become actively involved and push our elected officials into acting more like employees as opposed to employers. They work for us, we pay their salaries, let's act like that is the case.

Chapter 1

CRIMINAL COURT

And Justice for All, the 1979 film written by Barry Levinson, produced and directed by Norman Jewison. It stars Al Pacino as attorney Arthur Kirkland. Following is part of Attorney Kirkland's opening remarks to a jury in the film's final scene: "These proceedings are here to see that justice is done. And justice as any reasonable person will tell you is the finding of the truth...Let's go back to justice. What is justice? What is the intention of justice? The intention of justice is to see the guilty people are punished, and the innocent people are freed. Simple, isn't it? Only it's not that simple. However, it is the defense counsel's duty to protect the rights of the individual, as it is the prosecution's duty to uphold and defend the laws of the state. Justice for all. Only we have a problem here. And you know what it is? Both sides want to win. We want to win. We want to win regardless of the truth. Regardless of who's guilty or innocent. Winning is everything!" As opposed to an arena for competition our criminal courts system should be a fact finding exercise in pursuit of the truth. However, you get the justice for which you can pay. That axiom has been commonly accepted for more years than I can count. We have come to accept that high-priced mouthpieces, sharks or shyster lawyers can be the difference between a verdict of guilty or not guilty. In our current system, not guilty does not always mean innocent. There is "guilty" and "guilty under the law." Public defenders are often viewed as substandard lawyers that could not make it to the big name private law firms. The "heavy hitters" command the big bucks and can manipulate the system in any manner necessary to ensure an acquittal or substantially reduced penalty for their clients. If the accused has enough money, he or she can buy their way into more desirable outcomes. The disparity of the resources available to the Public Defender's Office and the offices of large private law firms can be as wide as the Grand Canyon. Equally wide can be the disparity of resources between the prosecutor's office and those of private law firms. The attorneys may be equally talented, but the playing field is decidedly bent in favor of the side with the most resources—money. Additionally, the case load for the government attorneys, public defenders and prosecutors is clearly more demanding. Socioeconomic status can be a more determinant factor in criminal cases than the truth. In my opinion, this represents "separate but equal" justice. And of course, that weighs heavily in favor of the more affluent be it victim or offender, and this has become acceptable in our society. How can we be so accepting, so comfortable with this reality? Taxation without representation was not acceptable; separate but equal public accommodations are not acceptable; voting rights for male whites only is not acceptable; separate but equal justice is equally not acceptable. Our criminal courts have often been described as an adversarial system. Whichever side has the best presentation wins. Johnnie Cochran said, "If it doesn't fit, you must acquit." My assertion is that the criminal court system should be a fact-finding exercise in pursuit of the truth. Justice is attained only after the truth is revealed.

In 1982, James Ealy was convicted of the murders of Christine Parker and her three children. One of the three children, a three-year-old boy was sexually assaulted by Ealy. At the time of this incident, Ealy was on bond for a criminal sexual assault. Ealy's convictions were overturned by an appellate court, citing the police had no probable cause for his arrest. According to the police report, Ealy was briefly interviewed in his apartment and then invited to voluntarily come into a police facility for questioning. The officers did not draw their weapons, handcuff him or announce that he was under arrest. Ealy was advised his Miranda rights before questioning.

During the appellate hearing, the defense argued that Ealy was held for eighteen hours and given little opportunity to relieve himself; therefore, he was under arrest. Ealy signed a "consent to search" form for his bedroom, and the police recovered incriminating evidence therein. Ealy confessed to the crimes. With one dissenting justice, the panel of three judges overturned Ealy's convictions. Judge Thomas Maloney, who presided over Ealy's original trial, made this statement: "When this dangerous man is released from the penitentiary, the state should rent every billboard in the county and state to announce that he has been turned loose."

In December 2006, James Ealy was arrested for the murder of Mary Hutchinson. Mrs. Hutchinson was the manager of the Burger King at which Ealy worked. There is no amount of public outcry that can right this wrong. There is no way to hold culpable the police officers that arrested Ealy for the four murders in the Rockwell Gardens housing project in Chicago. We cannot formally assign blame to the appellate court judges that freed Ealy for what they interpreted as a violation of his constitutional rights. As a society, we have to swallow this outcome; we have to settle upon the fact that the family of Christine Parker received no justice for their losses. We have to grin and bear the fact that this "dangerous man" was free among us, and while free, he lawlessly took the life of Mary Hutchinson. We have to accept this because in our system of justice, following the rules is more important than justice for the victims of wrongdoing. We are encumbered with a system that fosters concealment of the truth as an acceptable strategy in criminal court proceedings. It appears that our criminal court system is more concerned with supporting its competitive nature as opposed to uncovering the truth and meting out justice.

In no way do I support a system that tolerates violating constitutionally protected rights. My concern is that our system provides opportunities for guilty persons to avoid the consequences of their crimes. We must call upon our Supreme Court to reverse Mapp v Ohio and eviscerate, dissolve, throw out the exclusionary rule. I understand its intent; it is critically important that law enforcement officials do not violate our constitutional rights. Police officers must be restrained; they must not be allowed to adopt a "by any means necessary" approach to enforcing the law. At present, when the officer makes a mistake, only the victim and his/her family suffer any consequence. The offender is freed of any responsibility, and at worse, the officer gets embarrassed in court. Law enforcement is more than a job, it is a sacred profession. The men and women that don those uniforms and report for duty every day have sworn an oath to perform some of the most difficult tasks required by our society. They must and should be appreciated. And they must and should be held accountable for every aspect of the service they provide. If/when a police officer makes a mistake while enforcing a violation of the law, that officer should be mandatorily disciplined by his/her agency for that mistake. Each man and woman that dons the uniform of a police department has attended a training academy and successfully completed the training. Each police officer has satisfactorily completed the required testing of that training academy AND passed a mandatory licensing exam required from the state in which they shall police. Many police agencies conduct roll call training daily. And in some police agencies, there is mandatory annual in-service training. Given these facts, there is no acceptable excuse for an officer to operate outside of department policy and state law. I recognize that each officer is human, and that there are NO perfect people. However, as police officers, we are held to a different standard given the awesome responsibility of that office. A matrix should be established with clear and determinate consequences for the various missteps an officer can make. There should be absolutely no variance for making these mistakes. However, there should never be any mistake that excuses the offender of the consequences of his/her deeds.

There have been occasions when law enforcement officials have committed crimes against the offenders they have arrested. There have been offenders that were physically abused as punishment for their crimes. Some confessions have been beaten and/or tortured out of arrestees. There is absolutely no excuse for this treatment, and the officers guilty of such should be prosecuted to the fullest extent of the law. But again, the crimes committed against the guilty persons should not excuse them from the legal punishment they should receive.

Utilizing the Criminal Justice System to address crimes committed against our citizenry is part of the bedrock of our society. Citizens are consistently urged to summon the police when they have been victimized. However, far too often, the victims do not attain the justice they seek and deserve. There exists jargon that states there is "guilty," and there is "guilty under the law." I submit guilty is ALWAYS guilty regardless of circumstances. There is absolutely no logical reason to excuse the crimes of any person because of actions or inactions by others. Everyone of sound mind must be held accountable for his/her actions. When the system fails to punish the offender, the victim is left feeling twice victimized. Victims are encouraged to utilize the system as opposed to seeking justice on their own. It is incumbent upon the system to adequately provide the justice the victim deserves.

720 ILCS 5/12-3.05 (ILCS...Illinois Compiled Statutes...The Criminal Code)

A person commits aggravated battery when, in committing a battery, other than by the discharge of a firearm, he or she knowingly does any of the following:

(1) Causes great bodily harm or permanent disability or disfigurement

One of the cases I handled as a Chicago police officer involved a woman being struck at the top of her head and down the right side of her face with a heavy glass ashtray. She suffered seventy-six stitches and lost use of her right eyelid. I made an arrest and attempted to secure the appropriate felony charge, aggravated battery. The assistant state's attorney in felony review rejected the felony charge which left me with no alternative but charging the offender with a misdemeanor offense. The details of this case are as follows:

Mary is a middle-aged homeowner and has been in her home for twenty-two years. She is a widow, and her children have moved out and are living their own lives. Her slightly younger brother Fred has fallen upon some difficult times, and Mary has allowed him to move in with her until he can do better. Pam lives on the same block and has been there at least fifteen years. Pam and Mary do not get along at all; they barely speak to one another and never visit with one another. Unbeknownst to Mary, Pam develops an interest in pursuing a personal relationship with Fred—she thinks he's really handsome. One summer evening, Pam decides to visit Fred as she wants to make her interest known to Fred. As it is summer, Mary's front door is open; the storm door is closed but unlocked. Pam brazenly opens the door and enters Mary's house. When Mary came to the door to question why she entered her home without at least the courtesy of ringing the bell, Pam responded, "I didn't come here to see you, I came to see Fred." In response, Mary told Pam that this was her house, and that Fred was just visiting. She instructed her to leave her home immediately and not to return. Pam responded that since she was there to see Fred that only Fred could make her leave. The two ladies began a verbal altercation during which Mary complained of spittle hitting her. Pam disregarded her complaint and continued yelling; Mary threw a half cup of water at Pam. Pam responded by grabbing a large glass ashtray from the inn table and striking Mary at the top of her head above her right eye and down her face to her cheek. As previously stated, it took seventy-six stitches to treat Mary's wound, and her right eyelid will never again close completely. When I questioned the assistant state's attorney about refusing the felony charges, he responded that since the victim was not admitted into a hospital, he could not justify approving felony charges. As I reread the law, 720 ILCS 5/12-3.05, I failed to find any language that required the victim be hospitalized. That requirement completely escaped me, but it was offered as justification for this assistant state's attorney's refusal of felony charges.

720 ILCS 5/18-1

According to 720 ILCS 5/18-1, a person commits robbery when he or she takes property, except a motor vehicle from the person or presence of another by the use of force or by threatening the imminent use of force. According to the Illinois Compiled Statutes, this offense is a felony.

I responded to a call of a "battery in progress" and found a sixty-three-year-old male, black, five feet eight and approximately 160 lbs. It was approximately 10:30 a.m., and the victim had been forced into an alley, beaten and robbed. It was the first of the month and the victim, George, had just left the currency exchange where he had cashed his social security check. The victim was able to give me a fairly good description of the assailant, and I issued a BOLO (be on the lookout) over the radio. Several minutes later, an officer responded that he had detained an individual that fit the general description. I drove George to that location, and he positively identified the man as the person who robbed. The assailant had the exact dollar amount of George's check in his pocket. The assailant, Ted, was taken into custody and transported to our district station for processing. The assistant state's attorney on duty approved the felony charges, and Ted was officially charged accordingly.

Thirteen months later, this case proceeded to trial as Ted refused the plea bargain. Ted had a lengthy criminal history, and he was advised that this charge would result in some serious time in prison. On the day the trial was to take place, I reported to the courtroom and observed that George was present and awaiting trial. The assistant state's attorney that was to try the case summoned us into the rear of the courtroom for pretrial interviews. After interviewing George, she interviewed me. Midway through the interview with me, she stated that I was lucky that she was not in felony review the day this arrest was made. She went on to say that she would have never approved the felony charges as the victim doesn't speak well. It is extremely difficult to understand what he is saying, and he seems to have difficulty understanding simple questions. She concluded by saying that I should not expect much; she probably would not be able to win this case. I reframed from comment and went to the jury room to collect myself. Yes, she had REALLY angered me as I just could not understand her defeatist attitude. George was not a scholar, but George IS just as human as any other person. I feared this prosecutor would not make a sincere effort to secure this conviction. I could not conceive why given the evidence we had, securing a conviction in this matter would be extraordinarily difficult.

Ted opted for a bench trial, and an hour later, he was found guilty of strong armed robbery. After the proceedings were complete, I could not completely restrain myself. I approached this assistant state's attorney and told her that I was oh so very happy that she was not in felony review the day of this arrest. Had she been there, George would have been denied the justice he so richly deserved strictly because he was not very well educated and/or articulate enough to satisfy her.

I am not going to attempt to excuse the insensitivity demonstrated by the assistant state's attorneys in the scenarios I just described. However, I'd like to offer some insight. Many of us have developed an image of our Criminal Justice System based upon stellar television dramas like NBC's *Law & Order*. During my policing career, I cannot tell you how many times I heard, "I know my rights, I watch *Law & Order* every week." I would then have to explain there's television, and then there's real life. Welcome to reality. The assistant state's attorneys in television dramas are assigned a case, one case and spend hours investigating this case and preparing for the impending trial. They leave the office and go out into the field and conduct their own private investigations and have time enough to bring charges against the actual offender as oftentimes the police arrested the wrong person. This makes for good fictionalized drama, emphasis on fictionalized.

In criminal courts all over this country, every Monday thru Friday, the prosecutors and public defenders enter courtrooms at approximately 8:30 a.m. Pushing a cart carrying at least thirty files, those files represent the morning call—the cases that will be heard that morning. After lunch, the prosecutors and public defenders will enter the courtroom with the same cart bearing the same number of files. Only these are thirty different files than the thirty they had that morning. That is the afternoon call. Of course, this will vary from jurisdiction to jurisdiction, but the general idea is the same. These offices, public defender and prosecutor do not have the manpower and/or resources to investigate each individual case in the manner portrayed in our popular television dramas and movies. The harsh reality is for the most part, the criminal court system is operated like an assembly line. Due to the sheer volume of cases, there is an extraordinary emphasis on ensuring that cases do not come to trial. Attorneys on both sides of the aisle work diligently to reach plea agreements and keep the trial calendar at bare minimum. These same attorneys are evaluated by the number of cases that do not reach trial. Prosecutors must consistently secure a high conviction rate in order to maintain employment. It is critically important that their politician bosses are in position to report to their constituencies they have convicted a high volume of offenders. The politician boss must be in position to report that he/she has supervised a staff that has won convictions for the vast majority of the cases they've handled.

Our criminal court system is commonly described as an adversarial system, a competition. It is a system where opposing counsel is supposed to argue matters of fact before an unbiased magistrate in order to attain justice. More simply expressed, defense lawyers and prosecutors are pitted against one another in the presence of a neutral judge to determine the guilt or innocence of the accused. I invite you to pause for a moment and consider what you've just read. In my judgment, I've just described a competition, a contest. The arena for this contest is the courtroom. The primary objective in this arena is winning. Absent from that description is attaining justice. In my opinion, this should be a fact-finding mission in pursuit of the truth. Justice can only be meted out by uncovering the truth. The criminal court system should not be utilized and/or viewed an arena for competition. Civilized societies developed the court system as a vehicle for persons who have been wronged to redress their grievances in a civilized manner. Court systems were developed as an alternative to vigilantism; civilized societies recognized the need for a central justice system. Centralized justice systems are an essential component of each society.

In a system that is supposed to provide relief to those who have been wronged, there is no room for arbitrary exercise. And by that, I mean we should have never allowed our criminal court system to devolve into a competitive exercise. The winning side in criminal court is often determined by which side presents the most appealing case. The current culture of the American criminal court is one that promotes the idea that the proceedings held within are matters of competition. The participants refer to the results as wins and losses as though matters of trial are akin to athletic competition. And as any sports fan can tell you that "on any given Sunday," one competitor can defeat another. The primary game plan is affixing responsibility. Oftentimes, the defense seeks to absolve the accused by dodging responsibility as opposed to revealing there is no guilt, that the accused is completely innocent of the charges. Our system of jurisprudence provides a variety of pathways for the accused to eschew, dodge responsibility regardless of the truth. Much too often, our criminal court system serves as an enabler: it allows defendants to shirk responsibility for their misdeeds. Issues addressed in criminal court should not be viewed as games of chance. The outcomes affect the real lives of the persons involved in a manner significantly more important than the outcome of a football game. It is critically important that we move swiftly to change this culture of competition; that we make the priority, the purpose of our criminal court system the discovery of the truth.

I have previously discussed eliminating the exclusionary rule, the "get-out-of-jail free" card for otherwise guilty persons. I am advocating eliminating any impediment to the discovery of the truth; anything that shall absolve a mentally capable person of the responsibility of his/her actions. Consistent with that line of reasoning, I must state that the inane affluenza defense should be immediately vitiated. The idea that when people of wealth and privilege have not been raised to know that the laws of society apply to them is obscene and must be rejected. When persons of the opposite end of the socioeconomic scale are the product of bad or inadequate parenting, there is nothing to excuse them of their criminal deeds. If justice is truly blind, there should not exist any set of circumstances that favors one group from another. Perceived wealth and privilege should not excuse a person from the consequences of his/her actions. Redd Foxx once joked, "Follow an ugly kid home, and somebody ugly is gonna open the door and let him in." In general, ugly acting children go home to ugly acting adults. During my professional career, I have had to deal with a multitude of thirty, forty and fifty-year-old boys. As opposed to being raised, trained and nurtured by responsible caregivers, they were enabled to consistently dodge growing up and maturing into adulthood. These enablers retarded the natural maturation process and left the person woefully lacking any sense of responsibility. Absent a healthy sense of responsibility, these individuals often commit various crimes as they've developed an unreasonable sense of entitlement. Just as a toddler believes every bright, shiny object that catches his/her fancy should be provided simply because he/she wants it; these individuals believe they are entitled simply because they live. They completely lack the concept of WORKING for that which you want, earning things through sacrifice and hard work. It is truly tragic that there are parents that do not take seriously their responsibilities as parents. The foundation of any society is the family unit. I understand that our society has allowed that basic, essential foundation, the family unit to erode over the decades. Therefore, we must reinvest in the development and maintenance of the family unit, our most precious resource. It is from the family unit that our children, the future of our society evolves. One of the major factors in the problems of our society is the incessant need to find excuses for the failure of persons to meet their responsibilities. Our criminal code rightly protects persons that are truly unable to make rational decisions. If a person is born absent the ability to determine right from wrong, we must treat that person in a different manner. However, being the product of lousy parenting does not take away a person's mental ability to discern right from wrong. Since sociopaths and persons with antisocial personality disorders do not meet the criteria of being unable to discern right from wrong, spoiled rich brats do not meet it. There is a clear distinction between reasons and excuses. Reasons are circumstances that exist independently of any outside influence. Excuses are those things a person will reach for in an effort to avoid taking responsibility. A psychotic person does not choose his/her illness and is not responsible for that illness. The psychotic person is incapable of determining the difference between right and wrong. Those persons supposedly afflicted with affluenza know and understand the difference. They just choose not to comply with the laws and rules of polite society as they view said laws beneath them. "Got off on a technicality" should be forever stricken from our jargon. Our definition of justice should be centered upon uncovering the truth, lawfully but without exception. Justice cannot be attained in a system that supports the practice of dodging responsibility.

I have a healthy respect for the legal profession. Successfully completing law school and passing a state bar exam is one of the most challenging accomplishments there is. There is nothing about this book that is meant to marginalize any aspect of the legal profession. However, it is my intention to put to bed the mystique that surrounds criminal law. Part of my motivation for writing the exact language of the two offenses I described previously is to illustrate that there is no mystique, no ambiguity or gray area regarding criminal law. It takes only a high school reading equivalency to read and under-stand criminal law. I will again state this assertion is not an attempt to marginalize the legal profession or the rigors of law school. For those who doubt the challenges of completing law school, I invite them to take the Law School Admission Test (LSAT). I particularly invite them to focus on the part of that exam commonly referred to as logical games. If after doing such you are left with the impression that successfully completing law school is not a big deal, you should immediately enroll.

Most local law enforcement agencies require that candidates have completed at least two years of college; that requirement is fairly recent—last three decades or so. Initially, the minimum educational requirement for local law enforcement was a high school diploma or its equivalent. One of the primary duties of a police officer is to read, interpret and enforce criminal laws as they are written. Given that fact the rest of the populace should not be intimidated by criminal laws. There is a significant portion of our citizenry that can sit in observance of the daily proceedings in a criminal court and evaluate how effectively a courtroom is operating. In most jurisdictions, local judges are elected every four years. I submit that the vast majority of voters have little if any information about the individuals seeking election to judge. Most of the people elected to judge are done so because they've been slated by the dominant political party in that jurisdiction, not because the voters have properly vetted them. We must maintain the distinction between the three levels of government: executive, legislative and judicial. The idea of a politician/ judge is not at all appealing. However, these judges are elected, and we should have infinitely more information at our disposal before making that choice. I am proposing that citizens from neighboring jurisdictions be chosen to work as courtroom evaluators. It is important that they not work in their home jurisdictions so as to reduce the prospect of arbitrary biases. After being selected to work in this position, they will be trained to understand each nuance of courtroom procedure; but most importantly, they will have access to the criminal code. Given the fact that criminal laws are written such that only a high school reading equivalency is required to understand them, the pool of applicants should not be that narrow. The persons chosen to work in this capacity shall work in teams of three. They will be instructed not to share their respective evaluations with one another; the evaluations will remain confidential. Evaluations shall be submitted electronically at the close of business each day. The criteria by which each jurist is evaluated should be the same, it must be constant. Keep in mind that at present the first exam a prospective police recruit must pass in a reading comprehension test at a high school reading level. Each judge in the jurisdiction shall be evaluated quarterly, and the results of those evaluations must be made public. In fairness to the judges, they will be allowed to respond to the evaluations so as to counter any information he/she finds unfair or erroneous. The function of the local judiciary is much too important to be governed by the power brokers of the dominant local political party. Justice must be blind and not colored by any party affiliation.

I understand there are geographical issues regarding this suggestion. Using my hometown Chicago as an example, it is unreasonable to expect citizens from DuPage County to travel to Cook County courtrooms and vice versa. That commute during rush hour could be at least three hours. For the large metropolises, judicial territories can be established, and those persons seeking election to judge would have to choose the territory in which he/she wanted to serve.

The persons hired to evaluate the judges in a particular judicial territory would not live in that particular judicial territory. The agency charged with the responsibility of evaluating the judges must not report to any elected official. There should be a clear and obvious separation of management between this agency and the office of any elected official. I understand establishing this agency will incur a significant cost. I shall explain how that cost can be met later in the book. Transparency is critically important in this matter; we must be ever vigilant to ensure our courtrooms are not politicized.

Chapter 2

POLICE

The most visible extension of any local government is its police force. Providing policing services is an essential function of government. It can also be a lightning rod for controversy and discontent. There is no comparable function to policing. The women and men who choose this profession are unique and should receive our utmost appreciation and respect. Most complete their careers honorably and with little fanfare. However, as with any other part of our society, the officers that dishonor the badge receive the most attention. Police officers that violate their oaths of office, commit crimes and tarnish their badges should be exposed. Law enforcement professionals should be held to a higher standard, and anyone seeking a career in law enforcement should be accepting of this fact. Remember, you did not get drafted…you volunteered. And although respect and appreciation should come to members of a police force, respect and appreciation are earned.

Black Lives Matter. One of the most controversial movements of recent history is the Black Lives Matter initiative. This movement arose after a series of seemingly needless killings of black men by mostly white police officers. Our current technology (cell phone cameras and such) along with social media exposed these incidents on a global level. Eugene "Bull" Connor, public safety administrator for Montgomery, AL became an unwitting asset to the civil rights movement of the 1960s. The brutality he engineered upon unarmed and peaceful black people seeking to participate in the voting process was televised for the entire world to see. And faced with its ugly and despicable treatment of its own citizens, America had to address its own human rights violations as it continued to chastise other nations about the same. Thank you, Eugene "Bull" Connor. My mother provided all the information I needed regarding how I should handle "race relations" in the aftermath of the assassination of Rev. Dr. Martin Luther King, Jr. While we were watching the unrest and carnage on television that followed this tragedy, she pulled me aside and said, "I'm going to teach you about white people." I stood in anxious anticipation for the sage tutelage from my mother, and she continued, "All white people are…PEOPLE. You're gonna get good, bad, and in-between. If you automatically judge that because they are white they are against you, you're gonna miss some opportunities to meet and work with some people that can help you. On the other side if you automatically believe that all black people are with you, that they are on your side, you will set yourself up for hurt and disappointment. Allow each person to show you who they really are before you judge." The older I get, the smarter my mother was.

Some of the critics of the Black Lives Matter movement suggest its organizers are attempting to send the message that the lives of black Americans are in some way more valuable than lives of others. Perhaps if the organizers retitled their movement to Black Lives Matter TOO, it would satisfy those detractors. It is not now, nor has it been the objective of the Black Lives Matter movement to place the lives of black Americans in a position more valuable than the lives of any other group. The basic tenor in this nation, established in its infancy is that the lives of black people are less valuable than others. After the colonists declared themselves free of the British government and met to form a government, one of the points of contention was how the slaves would be counted. In order to establish dominance in the House of Representatives, the Southern states wanted the slave population to count toward the number of congressman that would represent their states. The Northern states argued that the slaves were considered property; hence, they could not be considered citizens.

The stalemate was overcome with the Three-Fifths Compromise. In the original version of this nation's Constitution, slaves were considered Three-Fifths, 60% human. In 1857, the U.S. Supreme Court handed down the Dred Scott decision that ruled in part whether a black person was enslaved or free he/she could not be an American citizen. Congress passed a Civil Rights Act in 1964 to protect people from discrimination in housing, public conveyances, education, etc. However, the Voting Rights Act of 1965 has to be revisited every five years. The most powerful tool a citizen will ever possess is the right to vote. Unlike the 1964 Civil Rights Act, the right to vote has to be periodically reaffirmed. I cannot identify any logical reason that the law which affirms each American citizen has the right to vote must be revisited EVER! D. W. Griffith's movie *Birth of a Nation* firmly implanted upon the nation's psyche the image of the super criminal/rapist black male. It even depicted members of the Ku Klux Klan as superheroes coming to the rescue of a nation in distress after these super criminals were let loose to beset the nation. In the 1988 presidential campaign, the Willie Horton ads for George H. W. Bush reversed the polls in his favor. The ads promised America that Bush would protect America, white America in particular, from super criminals like Willie Horton. President Bill Clinton introduced the "super predator" term while describing the criminal element he purportedly targeted. More recently, the governor of Maine, Paul LePage, has been quoted, "Guys with the name, D-Money, Smoothie, Shifty [who] come up from Connecticut and New York, they sell their heroin, they go back home [and] half the time they impregnate a young white girl before they leave." He went on, "90% of those pictures in my book, and it's a three-ring binder, are black and Hispanic people. Black people come up the highway, and they kill Mainers." Maine's Portland Press published FBI statistics showing the overwhelming majority of those arrested in Maine for drug offenses were white, 14% were black. It is incomprehensible to me that a person so clearly bigoted was elected to public office, but maybe not. There are those who decry, "When will you all get over it?" My response is we'll get over it when YOU get over it. The overall point that I am making is a major contributing factor to the strained relationship between black communities, and the police is this underline tenor that blacks are less than, not really worthy, somehow subhuman.

"It took me a long time and a number of people talking to me through the years to get a sense of this. If you are a normal white American, the level of discrimination and the level of additional risk. White parents don't have to teach their teenage boys to be extra careful when dealing with police. Because it's not part of your normal experience" (Newt Gingrinch, Netflix docudrama, the *13th* by Ava DuVernay, 2016). Aid to President Richard M. Nixon, John Ehrlichman states, "You understand what I'm saying? We knew we couldn't make it illegal to be either against the war or black, but by getting the public to associate the hippies with marijuana and blacks with heroin. And then criminalizing both heavily, we could disrupt those communities. We could arrest their leaders, raid their homes, break up their meetings and vilify them night after night on the evening news. Did we know we were lying about the drugs? Of course we did." Author Dan Baum published in *Harper's Magazine* and also featured in the 2016 Netflix docudrama, the *13th* by Ava DuVernay.

One of the unfortunate truths in this world is that the misdeeds of the few can taint and/or bring shame to the entire group. There clearly have been atrocities committed against black people in this country by police officers. Much of the brutality suffered by blacks at the hands of police officers has been racially motivated. And now in the twenty-first century, the technology exists to openly display these horrendous deeds on a global level. These scant few rogue police officers have cast a shroud over the majority of police officers who honorably serve and protect the citizenry of our great nation. "People love it when you lose, they love dirty laundry" (Don Henley, "Dirty Laundry," 1980). Bad news, tragedy, unspeakable acts, attract readers and viewers. The media prominently features the worst in us as the "bad news" items draw the most attention. Recently, the deaths of black people during confrontations with police officers, white police officers in particular, have fueled protests and protracted debates nationally. Many of these deaths have been captured on film either by bystanders or camera equipment from the police agency involved. Video evidence has become a more damning tool than it was at the time of the Rodney King beating. In spite of specious efforts by the Chicago Police Department, the video of the killing of Laquan McDonald became public, albeit one year later. Further investigation prompted the Chicago Police Department to file charges of filing false official reports against seven of the police officers on the scene of that shooting. Officer Jason VanDyke has been charged with murder in that case. Most objective observers of this incident failed to identify any point when McDonald posed a threat to Officer VanDyke or any other person at the scene. Hence, the use of deadly force could not be justified.

U.S. Supreme Court decision TN v. Garner struck down the common law "fleeing felon rule." Therefore, Officer Michael Slager in South Carolina cannot justify shooting Walter Scott as he ran away from him after a traffic stop. Officer Slager offered the "I was in fear for my life" defense as justification for shooting Walter Scott in the back as he ran away from the scene of the traffic stop. The fearful Officer Slager fired multiple times at a man that was fifteen to twenty feet away from him and running in the opposite direction. If in fact Officer Slager was "in fear for his life," law enforcement was an offensively poor career choice. Judge William Bennett in Marksville, LA determined that the assertions of officers Derrick Stafford and Norris Greenhouse were without merit in the shooting deaths of six-year-old Jeremy Mardis and his father Chris Few. These officers fired eighteen shots into the car in which Few and Mardis occupied during a traffic stop. Their reasoning was that Mr. Few's actions placed them in fear of their lives. The video evidence depicts events in stark contrast to those assertions. Recently, the Massachusetts State Supreme Court has ruled that black men who flee the police should NOT be considered suspicious as they have a legitimate reason to fear the police. Given the fact that black men are disproportionately stopped more often by police officers in Boston, this fear is justifiable.

Viewing black people as less than human is as old as this country. Jackie Robinson's acceptance into Major League Baseball, civil rights legislation, the election of Barack Obama, etc. has not put to rest an undercurrent of bigotry and hatred that seemingly has an eternal shelf life. We cannot legislate attitudes or beliefs: just behavior. When choosing people to serve our communities as police officers, it will always be difficult to identify all those who are afflicted with some type of bigotry—racial, ethnic, religious, sexual orientation, etc. We must, however, be ever vigilant in a continued vetting process so as to protect the citizenry as much as humanly possible from disease that is bigotry.

We must also be mindful that the door swings both ways. As previously stated, the police officers that have been dominating the news are the few rogue officers that shame their badges. Most of this nation's police officers serve with honor and commitment to their oath. Some go above and beyond and give of themselves in an uncommon manner. Officers like Lindbergh Askew, Jr. and Sherman Sampson of the Chicago Police Department. Both Askew and Samson volunteered their time to train and coach grammar school and high school boys in football, with an emphasis of securing college scholarships. Officer Askew established the Chicago Blitz Youth Football and Cheer Organization for kids ages six thru fourteen. Officer Sampson worked with high school boys in football. Through their efforts, Askew and Samson have helped dozens of young men and ladies attain college scholarships and a vehicle out of the crime-ridden, impoverished neighborhood in which they grew up. These men have given of themselves minus any fanfare or accolades. However, the lives they have touched are innumerable. There has not been much national attention given to Officer Bobby White in Gainesville, FL. Officer White, a male white, can be seen on Facebook engaging several black teens on a neighborhood basketball court. After kidding around with them for a while, Officer White told them that he would return the next day with backup. And boy did he bring BACKUP. The next day, Officer White brought Basketball Hall of Famer Shaquille O'Neal to assist him in the pickup game. Of course, this was a spectacular treat for the teens, and Shaq appeared to enjoy the kids as much as they enjoyed him. I personally salute Shaquille O'Neal for taking the time and giving of himself; many in his position have opted not to do such. Perhaps because this event did not involve any tragedy it was not nationally newsworthy. I am confident though the participants found that day quite special. There are countless police officers that give of themselves daily just because they have found it within their heart to do such. And we should celebrate them as much as we vilify the rogue officers that dishonor their badges and commit crimes against our citizenry.

Not long after I began my policing career, I decided to bring "Officer Friendly" back to the Chicago Public School down the street from my house. I had served as a community representative on the Local School Council for the Amos Alonzo Stagg Elementary School, and I was aware that "Officer Friendly" had not visited that school in years. With the assistance of the Neighborhood Relations Office of the 007 Police District, I began Officer Friendly visits at Stagg. I learned many things from the children, and I am confident that I was able to provide valuable information for them. I know that I earned a reasonable amount of trust as some of the children shared information with me regarding criminal activity. And then there was that one tragic incident.

The principal of Stagg Elementary called our district desk and asked if I was on duty that day. A situation had arisen at the school that she believed only "Officer Friendly" could handle. The desk sergeant sent a radio communication for me to report to Stagg Elementary School. Upon arrival, the principal met me at the door and explained she asked for me as she was convinced that only I could handle this situation. One of the teachers had found a suicide note written by a twelve-year-old female student. The note was addressed to this student's rape counselor. The young lady was visibly despondent and virtually noncommunicative. Her eyes were swollen from crying, and her clothing was in disarray. The principal had moved her into a small office, and I entered the room and sat with her. It did not take long before she began to tell me about her heartbreaking situation. She had a rape counselor as she had been raped by her mother's boyfriend. The boyfriend was tried, convicted and imprisoned for this crime. The child's mother blamed her for the boyfriend's crime. According to the mother, the girl lied about the whole situation; and even if the boyfriend had sex with her, it was because the child had seduced him. This was a Monday, and the girl had spent the weekend in Chicago Heights, a southern suburb of

Chicago, with her uncle and his family. According to the child, the uncle, her mother's brother, had raped her during that weekend visit. When she got home and told her mother of this crime, the mother became enraged and began calling the girl various tramps, liars and sluts. The mother told her that it was her fault that "her man" was in jail, and that she was not going to allow her to put her brother through that. I was able to reach her rape counselor, and through the Illinois Department of Children and Family Services, we were able to have this child immediately removed from that home. The Chicago Heights Police Department was notified, and a criminal investigation was initiated. I maintained communication with the rape counselor and later learned that the child was eventually placed with a loving foster family. In this instance, the dominos fell just right, and this child received the assistance she desperately needed. This instance made all the Officer Friendly visits worthwhile.

I understand the anger that many feel regarding the senseless killings of black citizens by police officers. It hurts a little more when the assailant, the assassin is someone that has sworn to protect you from harm. But there is nothing that can justify the ambush killings of police officers: it is wrong on every front. I understand the angst, the overwhelming anger that has overtaken the black community in this nation; everyone has a saturation point. But when emotion drives the decision making process, the emotion will ALWAYS bite you in the butt. The response to injustice has to be rationale IF it is going to be effective. Randomly killing police officers does not strike back at the guilty officers. The persons responsible for the murders are not affected by these random ambush killings. While doing such, can the perpetrator be assured he/she is not killing a Lindbergh Askew, Jr., Bobby White or Sherman Sampson? These cowardly acts serve only to further drive the wedge deeper between the black community and the police agencies every citizen needs. Poverty breeds crime, and given the fact that many of the most impoverished communities in this country are black communities, we NEED the police. Do not interpret this as though I am advocating that black communities in this nation should accept mistreatment and/or criminal acts committed against them by police officers. Socioeconomic status or any other status does not afford police officers a legitimate reason to victimize anyone. Conversely, there is no acceptable reason for citizens to target police officers for death.

I am a former United States Marine, and it is my assertion three months of Marine Corps basic training better prepared me for policing than six months in the Chicago Police Academy. When I arrived at Marine Corps Recruit Depot San Diego, CA on August 5, 1977, I never once doubted that this was going to be the most challenging experience of my life. And as it turned out, it was the most rewarding experience of my life. Not long after arrival, we were greeted with the message that not all of us were going to make it. The drill instructor went on to say that they were going to use every means fair and unfair to determine if we packed the gear to serve in his beloved Corps. He did not exaggerate. For the next three months, we were pushed to our absolute limits physically, mentally and emotionally. After viewing several popular movies such as *Full Metal Jacket* or *An Officer and a Gentleman*, some may conclude the physical aspects of Marine Corps basic training was the most challenging. Not so, the mental and emotional challenges were far more taxing. One of my most memorable days in training was when Senior Drill Instructor Gunnery Sergeant Stein began talking to us about leaving the emotion out of our duties in combat. He went on to say that emotion led to tunnel vision, and when tunnel vision takes over, you become a dead Marine. You need a panoramic view, an all-encompassing view of that with which you are confronted in order to survive, in order to win. Emotion clouds judgment and can lead to fatal mistakes. Logic and reasoning are the most effective tools a Marine has. As Marines, we are "mission oriented" and must be prepared to adapt, improvise and overcome to achieve our objective: complete the mission.

This skill, the ability to divorce myself from the emotion and allow logic and reasoning to guide my actions has benefited me in virtually every aspect of my life. The ability to put emotion aside and allow my rational mind to guide my actions has benefited me both professionally and personally. I cannot, will not purport that in each and every instance of my life, I have successfully put emotion aside. However, in the most stressful situations of my life I have. It is because of the training I received in Marine Corps boot camp I never fired a weapon at a person while policing in Chicago. I spent my career in arguably the busiest of the twenty-five police districts in Chicago, the 007 District, Englewood. "Danger's no stranger to an Englewood Ranger. I work in 007, where the REAL POLICE work." These are commonly accepted declarations in the Chicago Police Department. At times, I will joke the only thing for which I've never arrested a person is…TREASON. Anything else you can name; I've locked a person up for doing.

We must revise the process of selecting and training police officers; our current process is not as effective as we need.

Part of the process for being accepted into a police academy is successfully passing a written psychological test. According to forensic psychologist Dr. Gary Fischer of the University of Minnesota, this test shall give insight to the following characteristics:

1. Impulse control
2. General intelligence
3. Judgment
4. Ability to perform boring or tedious tasks
5. Reasonable courage
6. Honesty
7. Integrity
8. Personal bias or lack of bias
9. Ability to tolerate stress
10. What motivated the candidate to choose law enforcement as a profession
11. Dependability
12. Ability to deal with supervision
13. Appropriate attitudes concerning sexuality
14. Prior drug use

This test can range from 300 to 350 multiple choice questions. I estimate the test is basically 75-80 questions that are asked in a number of ways. Reportedly, this test screens out 5% of the candidates that complete it. As I reflect upon taking the test, I became insulted as I recognized I was being asked the same questions over and again. It was my impression that the test was to determine if I'd contradict myself, if I could consistently answer questions in the same manner. As I've read more about this type of testing, I've learned that these tests are supposed to give police agencies an insight into the character of candidates for admittance to their police academies. This test is supposed to provide insight into the candidate's ability to handle stressful situations and give the testing agency useful information concerning the candidate's character. I'd like to contrast that with methodology used by the U.S. Marine Corps. Day in and day out for three months, the Marine Corps puts its recruits in consistently stressful situations. As previously stated, the Marines push their recruits to absolute edge of their endurance physically, mentally and emotionally. It is my assertion that a person's true character shall emerge under extreme stress. I'm confident that the Marine Corps is aware of such which is why the training is designed in that manner. Furthermore, I assert that the multiple choice test may be useful in some manner; however, depending solely upon it is a woefully inadequate vehicle to screen out candidates that "don't pack the gear" to serve and protect our citizenry.

The Marine Corps ethos, "The Few, the Proud" should apply to all law enforcement professionals. When we arrived at Marine Corps Recruit Depot San Diego, CA we were told that not all of us would make it through the training. Part of the mission of the drill instructors was to ferret out those persons ill-equipped to be Marines. I submit the same standard should be applied to police recruits. Law enforcement training should be just as challenging, just as demanding as Marine Corps boot camp. And I mean "old school" not a politically correct Marine Corps boot camp. Political correctness has no place in Marine Corps basic training or Police Academy training. The communities in which the prospective officers shall be working are NOT politically correct and watered down. Providing a "not-too-stressful" pathway through training benefits the recruit in no way. Most importantly, the "Club Med" training does not expose those candidates bereft the essentials to be police officers. The training staff will not be able to identify those candidates who "don't pack the gear" to effectively serve their communities. Absent the grueling training of which I speak candidates like Michael Slager who become so terrified of persons running away from them they resort to deadly force may continue to become police officers…TRAGICALLY!

I recognize that the function of being a Marine and being a police officer are appreciably different. However, the discipline provided by Marine Corps training is invaluable; the fact that oftentimes, Marine Corps basic training exposes those persons lacking the necessities of taking on the responsibility of being a Marine is invaluable. I strongly believe that instilling Marine Corps discipline into our police training will yield an effective and efficient police force. Additionally, police training must emphasize that pinning the badge upon one's chest is not a realization of power. The power is in the law, the law an officer has sworn to uphold. A police officer does not take on power; he/she takes on an AWESOME responsibility. The selection and training process must be grueling; it must be challenging because it is critically important to learn if the prospective officer's shoulders are broad enough to bear the burden of this AWESOME responsibility.

The minimum age for acceptance into most police departments is twenty-one. I believe that at age twenty-one, most people are not quite mature enough to take on the responsibility of policing. The minimum age should be twenty-five unless the applicant has served at least three years in the U.S. military. Prospective recruits are required to meet certain physical fitness standards to be accepted into academy training. During the course of training, there are other physical fitness standards that must be met in order to continue training. And finally, there is a physical fitness test that the recruit must pass to successfully complete the training. And with many police departments, not all, but many graduation from the academy marks the conclusion of any physical fitness requirement. In some police agencies, there exists an annual voluntary physical fitness test and a monetary incentive for successfully passing it. However, given the nature of this career, I strongly believe physical fitness requirements should be mandatory for continued employment. Each member of the police department from patrolman up to and including the superintendent/

chief should have to pass a biannual physical fitness test. Yes, I do mean to include the executive leadership. "Leadership by example" and "Appearance commands respect." Clichés perhaps but people pay much more attention to actions as opposed to words. Those individuals that ascend into leadership positions within a police department should be THE model to which the rank and file aspires. Persons that could double for "Humpty Dumpty" should never be in position to lead a viable police force.

There are advantages for the officer when he/she is required to maintain a high level of physical fitness. The most valuable possession a person can have is good health. Regardless of one's financial situation, health will determine your quality of life. Most of America works a significant portion of its life looking forward to retirement and reaping the benefit of a lifetime of work. Poor health will stand in the way of enjoying that dream retirement. Physical fitness provides a degree of confidence which is invaluable for police work. I submit that a physically fit officer will not be as quick to escalate the amount and type of force he/she utilizes when affecting an arrest. The physically fit officer will encounter less instances of resistance as the arrestee will have a different perception of the officer. The offender will not be as confident that he/she can overcome the arrest with physical force.

The maximum age for any new police recruit should be thirty-five, and there should be mandatory retirement after twenty years of service. After twenty years of service, police officers should retire with an 80% pension. Yes, I mean 80% and regardless of rank. The demands of this essential function of government should command that type of pension. Each municipality will benefit from a younger and healthier police force. The pension benefit will attract and retain more quality applicants. One of the biggest faults with government is that it tends to be more reactive as opposed to proactive. Mass hiring of police officers by major cities is a common "answer" when there is a significant increase in violent crime. The elected officials push through the necessary legislation to hire more police as a signal to their constituents that they are responding to the latest crisis. I purport that a consistent flow of "fresh new blood" will be a more effective strategy.

Working in law enforcement is a noble and rewarding career opportunity. I cannot adequately describe the endorphin rush I experienced each time that I was able to help a person in need. As previously stated, I arrested people for just about any index crime that can be named. It was wonderful to take illegal firearms off the street and seize drug money. I particularly enjoyed the look on the face of the drug dealers from whom I seized $10,000 or more when I informed them they would be getting a visit from the Internal Revenue Service. Interacting with citizens on my beat and working with them to resolve issues of crime and disorder was oh so rewarding. And then there's being in the courtroom to hear the judge announce that the "guilty" defendant has been found guilty is a satisfying experience. I believe that we can do a markedly better job of selling the virtues of becoming a law enforcement professional to our youth. The mechanism is in place, we have to make a concerted effort to make this happen.

The Junior Police and Police Explorers are long-standing youth organizations offered by many law enforcement agencies. There is a relationship between those organizations and Boy Scouts of America. These types of youth organizations have been instrumental in assisting with the development of some of our youth. I propose an expanded effort to enlist more youths in Junior Police and Police Explorers. Several positive things can develop from this effort. Some of the youths will pursue careers in law enforcement. Each will have the opportunity to develop a better understanding of what "actual" police work involves. With better understanding, those who choose other career paths will be more amenable to working in partnership with their neighborhood police. The Junior Police and Police Explorers should serve as fertile ground for developing future police officers. There are those who believe that recruiting more people from their neighborhoods to become police officers in their communities will assist with bridging the divide between police officers and the communities they police. Involvement in Junior Police and Police Explorers can assist in guiding youths to avoid pitfalls that can sabotage career aspirations, policing or other professions and vocations. I suggest a strong recruitment effort by each of our police agencies all over the nation to accomplish this fete. Exposing our youth to the ideals and principles of public service benefits our nation immeasurably. To ensure there is no socioeconomic hindrance, the financial obligation for membership should be nominal at best. The Junior Police and Police Explorers should be a permanent part of the budget for every police department in our nation. Later in the book, I shall reveal how the revenue to support this effort can be generated.

During the last five years of my career in the Chicago Police Department, I worked as a field training officer (FTO). With the exception of one recruit, I was blessed with outstanding candidates for policing. Before I became an FTO, I observed a few recruits that made me question how they successfully completed academy training. I found myself pondering, "How on earth did this person get out of the academy? Did the instructors not recognize he/she has absolutely no business in this profession? After my experience with this recruit, I came to understand. I knew within the first hour of working with this recruit that law enforcement was a poor career choice for him. He began our initial conversation by telling me that he had never been particularly popular, but after being accepted into the Chicago Police Academy, his popularity rose exponentially. He went on to talk about the fact that he was invited to go to one of the local bars with guys that had previously not wanted him around. They encouraged him to "flash his badge" at the door to gain entry without paying the cover charge. I stopped him in midsentence and asked had he not been advised by instructors in the academy how foolish it would be to attempt to use his badge in that manner. I reminded him that the general orders of the Chicago Police Department forbid its members from accepting gratuities. Furthermore, as a recruit, using his badge to gain free entry into a bar is foolish even after one has finished the probationary period. Of course, the owners will give you free entry as they expect you shall act as security for the bar; that you will take immediate police action in case of a disturbance. Alcoholic beverages and the firearm are a toxic mix. I cautioned him that he found himself in a shooting situation, the mix of the alcoholic beverage and his firearm would almost surely sound the death knell for his career. Even after an officer has completed probation, alcoholic beverages and firearms are ALWAYS a bad combination. My immediate impression was that this recruit lacked the necessary judgment to effectively work as a police officer. Any person that could not recognize he/she only became popular after attaining police credentials does not have the necessary perception for police work.

Not long after we left the police station, we had occasion to stop in the strip mall for some foot patrol. I immediately observed a vehicle illegally parked in front of a fire hydrant and wrote the appropriate parking citation. We began our foot patrol, greeting citizens and having occasional chitchat with some of the merchants. Approximately fifteen minutes later as we approached our police car, the driver of the illegally parked vehicle snatched the ticket off his windshield and approached my "partner" and angrily asked why he had received this ticket. He went on to say that he was only in the store a few minutes, and that he should not have received this citation. My partner's response was, "Don't ask me, I'm just a recruit." The angry citizen turned to me to question the citation, and I responded that there is no time limit for parking on a fire hydrant. And besides, if you notice the time of the citation and look at your watch, you'll see you've been parked there much longer than five minutes. Of course, he was not at all happy with that response; but at that point, the ticket had been issued. When we got back into the car, I explained to this recruit that it was no one's business how long he had been a police officer. It didn't matter if he had been "on the job" a day or twenty years, his time as a police officer should never be a topic of conversation.

Approximately two hours later, we affected a traffic stop after we observed someone driving a van disregard a stop sign; well at least I observed the van run the stop sign. The driver failed to produce a valid driver's license and insurance, and I instructed him to exit the vehicle. There were two passengers in the vehicle and a faint smell of burning marijuana. Our (CPD) procedure requires that when a driver fails to produce a valid driver's license, that person must be taken into the police station to make other bond arrangements. In Illinois, law enforcement officers must either seize the valid Illinois driver's license, a bond card or have the driver come into the police station to post a cash bond. However, the driver must be in possession of a valid driver's license. After the driver exited the vehicle, I began searching him incident to this arrest. He was searched, handcuffed and placed into the rear seat of the police car. Afterward, we instructed one of the passengers to exit the vehicle as we were going to pat him down and depending upon the results of a name-check allow him to leave the scene. The passengers became belligerent and began shouting various profanities. One of the passengers directed questions at my partner (recruit), and he responded, "Don't ask me, I'm just a recruit." At that point, I immediately used my radio to call for assist units…I knew that I was alone. This recruit was completely useless in this situation. When the assisting units arrived, we discovered both passengers had active warrants.

At the conclusion of each tour of duty, FTOs are required to write an evaluation of their recruits. In the evaluation that I wrote of this recruit, I questioned if he had the necessary judgment and courage to successfully work as a Chicago police officer. By the end of the week, I knew that he did not. I knew some of the instructors at the academy, and I called to ask how on earth this guy was allowed to graduate. The response that I received was chilling. I was told that the instructors were not allowed to fail any recruit as long as he/she could pass the written test, physical fitness test and firearms qualification. It did not matter if the instructors observed that the recruits demonstrated a lack of courage or displayed negative personality traits. The objective of the academy was to get these recruited out and onto the street as soon as legally possible. The instructors were informed that it would be the responsibility of the field training officers to ferret out the persons that did not belong. That was one of the more sobering experiences of my career; it appeared that putting bodies into squad cars was the primary objective of the training academy. It was related to me that the city was more concerned with making good on the investment it had made in recruiting and training the recruits than the overall product. Admittedly, it is expensive to recruit and train a class of police officers. And it is good business practice to ensure their value is received in return for that investment. But I can't help but contrast that with the process of becoming a Marine. The Marine Corps makes a significant investment recruiting and training but measures the value in its investment by the quality of the Marine produced as opposed to the number of Marines produced. In a July 2015 edition of *The Wall Street Journal*, Zusha Elinson and Dan Frosch reported, "The 10 (ten) cities with the largest police departments paid out $248.7 million last year in settlements and court judgments in police-misconduct cases, up 48% from $168.3 million in 2010, according to data gathered by *The Wall Street Journal* through public-records requests." The article went on to detail that over a five-year span, these cities are paying out over a billion dollars due to incidents of police misconduct. Given these facts, it is much more cost effective for any municipality to ensure it has recruited, hired and trained police officers in the manner in which I suggest. The process is decidedly more stringent, but you get that for which you pay.

Regarding the recruit I've previously discussed, at the conclusion of his field training, I failed him. I prepared a detailed evaluation explaining why he did not possess the requisite tools to effectively serve as a police officer. This recruit was immediately transferred to a different police district where he was allowed to complete his probationary period. Not long after completing probation, he was partnered with a veteran officer in that district. They had occasion to respond to a domestic disturbance in a two-flat apartment building on the second floor. When they entered the residence, there were several people in the residence all of whom were in an agitated stated. The veteran officer attempted to quell the disturbance and ascertain the exact nature of the complaint. One of the persons in the apartment grabbed a large kitchen knife from the sink and began shouting threats at a family member. The once recruit immediately ran out the door and left his partner alone among this madness. The veteran officer made an emergency call for assistance (10-1…in Chicago), and several units responded. A sergeant responded to the call and immediately questioned the officer that fled the scene. He explained to the sergeant that he believed in that situation the appropriate response was for him to leave the scene and seek shielding, cover and call for assistance. Of course, that response was not well received. I later received a call from the veteran officer. He wanted to know how on earth I could have recommended this guy for permanent hire. He was quite shocked and disappointed to learn that I had not. I sent a copy of my evaluation to him, and he was blown away. You see the quantity of officers on the street as opposed to the quality is what was most important.

The process that I propose will ensure a consistent stream of qualified recruits that have been expertly trained and prepared to effectively serve their municipalities. The recruiting process will begin with the Junior Police and move forward to adulthood. I do not suggest that others who have not been in the "pipeline" be eliminated for consideration. However, I am confident that those persons who have been in the "pipeline" will be outstanding candidates for hire. The ultimate goal is to ensure there is a steady stream of qualified candidates for police service available, and that each law enforcement agency is adequately staffed. At present, we are in a reactive mode. When there is some spike in violent crime, the mayor and city council announce a significant hiring event to appease the masses. Proactive measures are considerably more effective; there should never come a time when any part of this nation is inadequately policed due to a lack of able-bodied officers.

I must reiterate that there are many more quality police officers than substandard police officers. My goal is to make it much more difficult for the substandard candidates to successfully complete training and become fully certified police officers. In most police departments, once the officer has completed probationary status, that officer begins to enjoy the full benefit and protection of the union. The labor history in this country supports the absolute necessity of organized labor. Unions are a must! The existence of labor unions in this country is an essential component to an effective workforce. The checks and balances attained with labor union involvement benefit all of America. It's what's rewarded that gets done. In general, people will provide an honest day's work for an honest day's pay. Tragically, there is a history of unfair labor practices in this country; hence the need for labor unions will never expire.

Whenever a police officer is accused of any type of infraction, the first call he/she will make is to the union. It is the responsibility of the union to provide legal representation for each of its members. The membership pays union dues for this benefit, and the union should provide the absolute best representation possible. The union should exhaust every avenue possible to protect one of its members from any unjust disciplinary measures. It is the duty of the union to provide such. However, in the case of a Michael Slager, who CLEARLY committed a crime, there should be no press conferences extolling the virtues of the accused. Every person is entitled to a defense, and the union should protect the rights of the Michael Slagers of the world. However, the union should be careful not to appear supportive of clear and obvious transgressions/crimes committed by any of its members. Rushing to judgment should never be a strategy employed by any entity, but in cases like Slager's murder of Eric Gardner or the brutal Rodney King beating, a union will lose all credibility should it attempt to justify those actions. The union owes its majority membership that performs their jobs capably and ably a never-exhausting effort to make clear that there is no tolerance for police misconduct.

Ladies and gentlemen, there is NO legal right to resist arrest. Regardless of the situation, you do NOT have the right to resist arrest. If in fact the arrest has no legal justification, the point of arrest is not the venue in which that fight should be fought. You cannot win that fight on the street; you can only worsen your circumstances. If you are being unjustly arrested, there are checks and balances in place that you can use to attain justice. When a person is being mistreated, wronged or abused, the natural first reaction is to cry out, protest and/or resist. However, when dealing with a police officer on the street, conducting one's self in that matter will almost always work against you. And besides, at times the officer could very well be making a lawful arrest, and you are just unaware. Our news media should seek to assist in this matter as this information should become more commonly disseminated. Additionally, the news media should eviscerate the use of the oxymoronic term "routine traffic stop." Routine traffic stops are as real as unicorns. One of the most dangerous activities performed by police officers is a traffic stop. Significant numbers of police officers are killed or injured during traffic stops each year. The news media must cease poisoning the minds of the public with this ridiculous characterization.

One of the arrests I made during my career speaks directly to this matter. This involves a DUI arrest. When this case came to court, the young man I arrested came to court convinced that this arrest was not valid. He believed he had been falsely arrested and he was anxious to have his day in court. When the clerk called his name he raced his lawyer to the front of the courtroom and confidently announced, "This is a bogus arrest, he can't lock me up for DUI; I wasn't drinking, I was just smoking weed." The judge responded, "Excuse me." And the young man repeated, "I wasn't drinking, I was just smoking weed." The judge's response this time completely startled the young man and some of the other young people in the courtroom. The judge stated, "Well we don't have to go any further with this case. I'll see you here in a month and inform you of what your sentence is." The bewildered young man stood there with a blank stare and the judge informed him that he had pronounced his guilt in this matter and that only the sentencing aspect of this case was left to complete. The defense attorney took the young man aside and explained that DUI is not driving drunk; it is driving under the influence. In the State of Illinois, if a person is driving with any amount of illegal drugs in his/her system, that person is guilty of DUI.

Many times during the course of my career, I was told by a citizen, "I know my rights, I watch *Law & Order* all the time." And yes, that would give me plenty about which to laugh. In my opinion, *Law & Order* is an excellent television drama; however, it is not a dependable reference for actual criminal law and procedure. The legendary attorney Clarence Darrow once quipped, "A man who is his own lawyer has a fool for a client." It is not my intention to declare that the general public is completely clueless regarding matters of criminal law and/or their individual rights. And I strongly encourage any person to pursue appropriate action in the event he/she believes their rights have been violated. However, I cannot overemphasize that the point of police action, the street, is not the place to adjudicate such. If the situation is not overly tense, requesting the presence of a supervisor is a viable option. But in certain situations, the most prudent move is to wait until legal counsel can be secured. Utilizing the Internal Affairs department of that police department or an existing citizen's review board is preferable to attempting to win an argument with a police officer on the street.

In an article published in the *New York Post* on December 27, 2016, Heather McDonald wrote: there had been 4,334 people shot in the City of Chicago as of that date. Of the 4,334 people shot, 25 or 0.6% was shot by police officers. Overwhelmingly, many more black people in Chicago were killed by other black people than killed by police officers. During 2016, Chicago suffered more homicides than New York and Los Angeles combined. In 2011, the Ku Klux Klan released the following letter:

The Ku Klux Klan would like to take this time to salute and congratulate all gangbangers for the slaughter of over 4,000 black people since 1975. You are doing a marvelous job. Keep killing each other for nothing. The streets are still not yours, nigger…It is ours. You are killing each other for our property. You are killing what could be future black doctors, lawyers and businessmen that we won't have to compete with. And the good thing about it is that you are killing the youth. So we won't have to worry about niggers in generations to come. We would further like to thank all the judges who have over sentenced those niggers to prison. We are winning. And pretty soon, we will be able to go back to raping your women because all the men will be gone. So you gangbangers…keep up the good work. We love to read about drive-by shootings. We love to hear how many niggers get killed over the weekends. We can tolerate the nigger's jungle fever (for now) because that further breaks down the race. Without the men…your women cannot reproduce. Unless of course, we do it for them, then we will have successfully eliminated a race—thanks to your help and commitment to killing each other. If most of you nigger gangbangers cannot read this letter, it is okay. Go pull a trigger and kill a nigger. It was critically important for slave owners, the Ku Klux Klan and other bigots to dehumanize blacks: that made it feasible, comfortable to brutalize and mistreat black people in that manner. However, we contribute to this abomination by mistreating one another. In fact, one can argue that we are crueler to each other than others are cruel to us. As the Klansman stated and statistics illustrate, we kill more of us than any other entity. We decry blatant bigotry from others, but we grease the skids by the manner in which we treat one another: refer to one another.

"Nigger" is a degrading and hateful word regardless of who utters it. Anyone can rationalize just about anything, but the truth is the light. My feelings toward the word changed decisively by listening to Richard Pryor. Yes, Richard Pryor. You will find no bigger fan of Richard Pryor than me, and I've laughed violently at his stand-up performances. It was in his film, *Richard Pryor: Live on the Sunset Strip* where he changed my mind about this heinous word. He spoke of his visit to an African nation, and the fact that while he was there, the word had not entered his mind. He concluded that he had been WRONG for so long, and that he would never again use that word. That declaration gave me cause for pause. And I encourage EVERY black person to rethink this: I encourage black people to begin to demonstrate you care more for one another than material things. Until we consistently demonstrate that we actually love ourselves, we will never garner the love and respect we so richly deserve from others. And while it is true that there are many too many instances where black people are mistreated by law enforcement, there are exponentially more cases that we mistreat each other.

On one occasion in the 007th Police District, an eight-year-old child was killed by rifle shot during a gang fight outside her home. It was approximate 3:00 a.m., and she was asleep in her bed. The following week, another gang fight occurred at approximately 2:00 a.m. one street east of that location. One of the gang members was using an AK-47 assault rifle. Many of the homes on that block are frame houses—the type of homes rifle shot will tear through like a hot knife through butter. Several police officers responded to the numerous calls, and the perpetrator was shot and killed in a firefight with police officers. Later that morning, six to eight protestors picketed the 007th District Police Station.

I completely understand the genesis of the Black Lives Matter movement. However, I must suggest that it can gain even more credibility should it call to task black people. Black lives must matter to black people, and sadly, there is overwhelming evidence that a significant number of black people do not share that sentiment. I suggest that the leaders of the Black Lives Matter movement organize a nonprofit organization and work to build this movement. Successful organizations are built around ideals and principles as opposed to individuals. The crisis of black people being disproportionately murdered in this country is not a fad. This issue will not dissipate in a matter of months. There must be long, hard work put in to effectively address this matter. It is an undeniable fact that this country owns a history of police brutality against its black citizens, and since it is the responsibility of the police to protect all of the citizenry, this betrayal is most hurtful. Police unions should not seek to provide safe harbor for officers such as Officer Betty Shelby as they are selfish individuals. Selfishness is a dangerous trait; selfish officers such as Michael Slager are not dependable and will put the lives and careers of other officers in jeopardy. These officers intentionally and recklessly break the rules of their departments, violate the laws of the state and then expect fellow officers to falsify official reports to cover their lawlessness. The Black Lives Matter movement and other protests seek to address this matter. But I must ask: where are the protests, calls to arms and meaningful movements to address the fact that we are killing ourselves at a far greater rate than rogue police, the Ku Klux Klan, American Nazi Party or Skin Heads? As with most situations in life, the "few" are the crux of the problem: the primary reason the problem exists. We cannot sit in fear of those few incorrigibles in our community and then vilify all of our police officers for the crimes and missteps of the few. In fact, I propose that the Black Lives Matter movement should seek to work in partnership with the local police unions to address these matters. The police unions will be well served to emphatically state that there is zero tolerance for brutalizing any and all citizens. The unions have an obligation to protect the majority of its membership from the negative consequences generated by the criminal acts of the "few." Members of the

Black Lives Matter movement must address all sources of the senseless killings of black people. Furthermore, Black Lives Matter should condemn the cowardly, ambush killings of police officers. Working in partnership, police unions and the Black Lives Matter movement can form an effective and efficient relationship. Both entities can benefit mightily from the trust and respect they will formulate in this proposed partnership. There is absolutely ZERO benefit in a divide between police and the black community or any other community in our nation. Given the occurrence of index crime in black communities working in partnership with police agencies is the most effective strategy to improve the quality of life in these crime-ridden neighborhoods. I strongly urge police unions nationwide to initiate this partnership; it must be initiated by the rank and file. This type of outreach by the "brass" can be construed as politically motivated and disingenuous. The officers on the street and in the communities can earn the trust necessary to grow this invaluable partnership. And in turn, the citizenry must be receptive to outreach from its police officers. Community leaders, clergy and all peace-loving citizens, prepare your hearts and minds for embracing the members of YOUR police department. Police officers are essential threads in the fabric of any successful and thriving community. When good, honorably serving police officers are murdered, citizens throughout the municipality should be outraged. My friend and co-worker Eric Lee was murdered by a drug dealing, gangbanger, and there was ZERO outcry from the community he so ably and honorably served. The whole community is adversely affected by the loss of stellar officers like Eric Lee. It should be a time of mourning for the community as a whole when they are stolen from us.

When the City of Chicago decided to move toward community-based policing in 1993, Chicago Alternative Policing Strategy (CAPS) some veteran officers were more than a little skeptical. Grizzled veteran police officers were not ready to accept a new philosophy in policing. They were accustomed to the US v. THEM attitude that had guided their entire careers. I was at the beginning of my career and working in partnership with the community was an appealing strategy. When Deputy Superintendent Charles Ramsey came to our district to announce that we would be one of the five test districts for CAPS, I became excited. During his address, he spoke of how our district, 007th, had approximately 70,000 residents, and that approximately 10% of the population of this district committed 85% of the major crimes. He told us that an outside agency would provide training for this new policing strategy, and I was chomping at the bit to get started. The training that was provided left a lot to be desired. The agency explained that our goal was to form partnerships with the residents and businesses on our beats, but the strategy for doing such was much, much too abstract. There was absolutely no substance to the training provided. Hence, I developed my own strategy to achieve the goal set before me. I am not a gadgets guy. I am in no way impressed by new electronic devices. Therefore, it was a huge step for me to go out and purchase a pager. Yes, I said it buying a pager was a gargantuan leap for me. The pager I purchased came equipped with a voice mail function, and I had business cards printed. As per instructed, I made sure that I "got out of the car" and met and greeted various residents on my beat. I began distributing my business cards and emphasized that it was possible to leave anonymous messages on the voice mail of my pager. Initially, the messages that I received were sparse; but as the issues were addressed, I received more and more messages. Most of the messages came from middle-aged and elderly people; the homeowners on the beat that had been in the community for decades. I addressed those issues that I could in a marked police car. Other information I passed onto the plain clothes officers (tactical unit) in our district. The more arrests the tactical officers made the more information I received. We were able to establish effective partnerships: the community with its beat officer, the beat officer with district tactical officers and issues of crime and disorder were summarily handled.

"An ounce of prevention is better than a pound of cure." It has been my longstanding belief that it is better to prevent crime than it is to solve crime. Poverty does breed crime as people will resort to crime to obtain the resources necessary to eat, house and clothe themselves. Of course, there is crime committed to attain certain luxuries and status symbols: there is no cookie cutter model to identify all criminals. However, I believe that a significant amount of crime can be abrogated via economic opportunity. Given that belief, I developed a strategy to address such. The Plumbers Union headquarters is virtually next door to the Fraternal Order of Police (union) headquarters in Chicago. While visiting the FOP Headquarters, I observed a flyer announcing a test to secure a job as a plumber's apprentice. I came to know that this was an annual event. I had never before seen this flyer, and after some investigation, I learned that this opportunity was not widely disseminated. I gathered a few of the flyers and took them with me. The next day when I began patrolling my beat, I began MY form of police harassment. When I saw a few young people gathered together, I stopped the car, ordered them to the nearest fence as though my partner were going to perform a stop and frisk. The young men, strictly out of some sort of muscle memory, immediately raised their hands and began spreading their feet apart. My response was to instruct them, "Put your hands down. This is not a stickup. What is happening to you is MY form of police harassment. "I began distributing copies of the flyers announcing the plumbing apprentice opportunity. We went over the instructions; there is an application fee and a test booklet that is provided once the fee is paid. Each successful applicant is required to pass an entrance examination. We went over the various phases of the career path to become a fully licensed plumber. And then I told them that it was illegal to be unemployed on my beat, and they could look forward to future "police harassment" like this. I went on to tell them that every time that I became aware of employment opportunities, they could count on being harassed like this. They were mostly stunned. One asked why we were doing this. My response was that if you get a REAL job, you will not have time to commit crime. You'll be much too busy at work and then resting when you get home from work to commit crime, and that will make my job much easier. From that point forward, I made a habit of enforcing MY form of police harassment.

As I reflected, I came to understand just why the initial instruction in community policing was so abstract. Each officer, each community has its own personality, its own needs. There is no cookie cutter blueprint for successfully and efficiently developing the requisite partnerships to police a community. However, the initial effort must come from the officer(s) assigned to that community. Police officers must seek to earn the trust of the citizens they are policing and ensure the citizens they need their assistance. The good guys DO outnumber the bad guys, and if we work in concert, we can overcome issues of crime and disorder in our communities. But we MUST work in partnership; we MUST establish trust. On a small scale, I have personally experienced the success of working as a team to overcome daunting circumstances of crime. I do not purport myself as being "super cop" or anything remotely similar. But since it worked for me in the community in which I worked, it CAN work for any dedicated, committed police officer.

The promotional practices in most police departments can use an overhaul. Much too often, deserving officers are passed over simply because they are not "in the car"... "one of the favorite sons or daughters"... in short, they don't know the "right" people. This age-old reality has adversely affected the overall morale of police departments for decades. It contributes to ineffective police work as the best and brightest can be left behind while less qualified officers ascend to positions of leadership and authority. Given that reality, our cities and towns are cheated: we fail to benefit from the true assets our police departments possess. Our police departments will operate appreciably more effectively when favoritism in the promotional process is eliminated. Given the fact this practice is so intrinsically engrained in the fabric of police departments, it appears the only way to eliminate such is to completely strip the departments of involvement in the promotional process. This responsibility should be awarded to independent agencies from outside the sphere of influence of the home municipality. For example, an agency from Delaware should administer the promotional process for the San Francisco Police Department. An agency from Florida should handle promotions for the police department in Detroit. The elected officials in our municipalities have demonstrated they cannot be entrusted with this responsibility. Police departments can be patronage playgrounds for certain elected officials.

In 1998, Mayor Richard Daley's appointment of Terry Hilliard as superintendent of Chicago Police surprised many. The odds on favorite appeared to be Deputy Superintendent Charles Ramsey. Ramsey was the perceived favorite after his stellar effort in implementing the Chicago Alternative Policing Strategy (CAPS). Ramsey appeared to be the darling of the day: the first-class show horse and clearly the next superintendent. And then this happened: during an interview with the *Chicago Tribune*, Ramsey was asked about his immediate goals if he became superintendent. One of his stated goals was to consolidate the bureaus. The Chicago Police Department is comprised of five different bureaus, each headed by "appointed" exempt rank bosses. "Appointed," in other words, the mayor's patronage playground. A few days later, Mayor Daley announced that Terry Hilliard was his choice: Charles Ramsey retired from the Chicago Police Department and went on to become Chief of the Metropolitan Police Department in Washington, D.C. In 2008, Charles Ramsey became the Commissioner of Police in Philadelphia, PA. Terry Hilliard retired after thirty-eight years of service in the Chicago Police Department. Hilliard currently heads up a consulting firm that reportedly is having difficulty earning a contract with the City of New Orleans. Supposedly, the biggest hang up is the perceived lack of voracity on the part of Hilliard in the investigation of former chief of detectives, Jon Burge. After Hilliard retired, Burge was convicted of perjury during an inquiry to his supposed reign of torture tactics in various black communities. The statute of limitations precluded any possibility of prosecuting Burge for the plethora of tortures he allegedly oversaw.

Chapter 3

SEX CRIMES

RAPE! Imposing one's self by force, the threat of force, taking advantage of an incapacitated person, preying upon a person that cannot reasonably consent to the ultimate form of intimacy is one of the most heinous crimes that can be committed. Tragically protecting people from this abomination is one of the most controversial aspects of our criminal justice system.

Chapter 720 ILCS 5/11-1.30: Aggravated Criminal Sexual Assault

A person commits aggravated criminal sexual assault if that person commits sexual assault and any of the following aggravating circumstances exist during the commission of the offense or, for the purposes of paragraph (7), occur as part of the same course of conduct as the commission of the offense:

(1) The person displays, threatens to use, or uses a dangerous weapon, other than a firearm, or any other object fashioned or used in a manner that leads the victim, under the circumstances, reasonably to believe that the object is a dangerous weapon.

Above is exact wording from the Illinois Compiled Statutes that describes the offense of aggravated criminal sexual assault. I am next going to relate to you a case that I personally handled in December

1993. I believe that it is important that you have this information as you read the particulars regarding this case.

For the purposes of this book, I shall not use the real names of the persons involved. This involves an allegation of rape and utilizing actual names is inappropriate.

At approximately 12:20 a.m., my partner and I responded to a call concerning an alleged victim of rape. This was a particularly brutal winter night in Chicago. There was a foot of snow on the ground, and the wind chill factor was -20 degrees. We found our complainant on the street a few feet from the pay phone from which she made the call. We met Pam; she was twenty-one years of age, five feet three, 115 lbs., on crutches with a broken foot. She was sobbing terribly and shivering in the artic Chicago cold. We asked her to sit in the back of the police car as we believed it would be considerably more comfortable. As Pam composed herself, she began explaining why she had called the police. Pam lived with her mother approximately four blocks south from where we were. She and her mother had been involved in a heated argument, and Pam decided to take the seven-block walk to her sister's apartment to get away from her mother. In the heat of the moment, that appeared to be a prudent idea; but very quickly, the reality of Chicago winter exposed that idea's flaws. Pam realized that she needed to quickly take shelter. She also knew that she was not far from the apartment home of one of her buddies, Tom.

She had known Tom for several years, and they had a good, friendly relationship. They were never romantically involved, and pursuing a romantic or intimate relationship had never been an issue. However, Pam felt comfortable with the idea of stopping by unannounced for the purpose of temporary shelter on her way to her sister's residence. Tom lived on the first floor of this two-flat apartment building and welcomed Pam into the apartment without hesitation. Pam stated that Tom had a guest. Paul, a person with whom she was not familiar, was there visiting with him. Pam related the circumstances of the argument with her mother to Tom, and the three of them laughed and talked about other things. Just as Pam believed she was sufficiently warmed and ready to complete her travels to her sister's apartment, she attempted to leave the apartment. Pam stated Tom and Paul had been whispering with one another, and Tom grabbed a baseball bat and blocked her exit from the apartment. Tom went on to inform Pam that she could not leave the apartment until she consented to sex with both he and Paul.

After Paul and Tom were finished with Pam, they allowed her to leave. The pay phone from which she called the police is approximately one hundred feet from the residence where she was violated. We asked Pam if her assailants were still at the residence, and she replied they exited the residence and walked north from this location. As a matter of protocol, we had to ensure Pam was taken to a hospital, and the most expedient path to the nearest hospital was to drive in the same direction as Pam's assailants. My partner and I surmised that the two bad guys had taken the two-block walk to the liquor store. (In "certain" communities in Chicago, liquor stores can obtain licenses to remain open until 4:00 a.m.) And of course, just as we approached that liquor store, Mutt and Jeff came diddy boppin' out of the store, bottle of liquor in hand. Pam immediately recognized them and indicated that we should stop. We stopped, called for assistance and took the offenders into custody. One of the assist units transported Pam to Holy Cross Hospital, and our arrestees were separated and transported to the district station for processing. When we arrived in the district station, I made the required telephone notification to the violent crime division of our detective unit. (At that time, there was no Special Victims Unit.) After which, I read the Miranda warning to Tom and asked if he wanted to answer any questions. Tom assured me that he understood his rights, and he was eager to talk. After being informed that he had been arrested for raping Pam, Tom was eager to talk. He stated that he and his friend did not rape Pam. His assertion was that Pam had come by to trade sex for drugs. Tom stated that he "sold a little rock on the side" to help him get by. Tom's story was that Pam came by to get some rock, but that she didn't have any money. According to Tom, Pam offered sex in exchange for a rock. After conferring with my partner, I came to know that between the two arrestees, they had $7.00: a paltry sum for drug dealers. I then began a new conversation with Tom. I informed him that Pam was at the hospital, and after being examined, we'll have a much clearer picture of what type of sex occurred between she and the two of them. Tom related the sex may appear to be rough because they used Glad sandwich bags in lieu of condoms. I assured him that we were much more interested in learning the "truth" about what happened as the alleged charges were too serious to treat the matter cavalierly.

At that point, I was able to secure a signed "consent to search" form from Tom and the keys to his apartment. I contacted an evidence technician, and we went to Tom's apartment to gather whatever evidence was present. Upon entering the apartment, we immediately observed the baseball bat of which Pam spoke, on the floor, on our right. As we approached the sofa in the living room area, we observed two Glad sandwich bags on the floor each containing what appeared to be semen. The sofa was out of place, the embarkations in the carpeting indicated such. The evidence technician collected the baseball bat and Glad sandwich bags, took pictures of the displaced sofa and carpeting. We then looked all over the one-bedroom apartment for any evidence of drugs, drug use or drug paraphernalia: we found nothing of the sort. There were no baggies for packaging the crack rocks, not a scale for weighing the drugs, no pipes for smoking, and there was no stash of cash that was earned from selling the drugs. After our search, we went back to the district station to complete additional paperwork and await the arrival of our victim.

At approximately 2:30 a.m., the investigating detectives arrived in the station with our victim. They informed me the results of the rape kit indicated the victim suffered injuries consistent with non-consensual sexual intercourse—RAPE. Additionally, as part of her medical work-up toxicology tests were ordered. As a favor to the detectives, a rush was put on the test, and the results were negative. There was no evidence of illegal drugs in the victim's system. Standard protocol for any allegation of rape requires that a criminal background check be conducted on the complainant. The purpose of conducting such is to learn whether or not the complainant has a history of prostitution. Of course, it is possible for a prostitute to be raped, but there are many occasions when prostitutes cry rape only when they do not receive payment for services rendered. The criminal background for Pam revealed that she had been once arrested for disorderly conduct and on another occasion arrested for retail theft. There was nothing in her criminal history regarding drugs or prostitution. The detectives took their turn interviewing our arrestees. Paul was as cool as the other side of the pillow. He stated that he had come over to visit his friend Tom and was surprised when Pam came to the door. He stated that since the weather was so bad and it was late at night, he did not expect any visitors. Paul denied being a "dope boy," but he insisted Pam came to the apartment to trade sex for drugs. Paul went on to say Pam begged Tom for a rock and agreed to sex with both men in exchange. Tom gave Pam the "rock," and she quickly smoked it. After smoking the "rock," it was time to pay up. When asked about the bat, Paul denied any knowledge of the bat. He stated that he didn't know that Tom owned a bat. After sitting in on that interview, I sat in on the interview with Tom. When I entered the room, Tom exclaimed, "You found those sandwich bags, didn't you?" I replied that he should calm down and answer the detective's questions as best he can. Tom repeated a story similar to the story offered by Paul; and we, the detective and I, left the interview room.

The next step was for one of the detectives to contact the assistant state's attorney in Felony Review and discuss with that person the findings and whether they believed pursuing felony charges was merited. The detective shared with the assistant state's attorney all the evidence that had been collected, the physical evidence collected from Tom's apartment, the results of the rape kit and the toxicology results. The assistant state's attorney decided that a visit to the district station was warranted. We all sat in the station until 9:00 a.m. or so when the assistant state's attorney arrived. During the wait time, I sat with Pam and assured her that we had collected more than enough evidence to move forward with the felony charges. I consoled her and repeatedly assured her that Tom and Paul would not escape punishment for the heinous crime committed against her. For the purpose of this book, the assistant state's attorney that arrived in our district station was Sue.

When Sue arrived, she immediately asked to review all the reports that had been completed regarding this case. She wanted also a print out of Pam's criminal history. Sue reviewed the documents and then sat with Pam to hear her side of this story. Keep in mind, Pam has told this story to me and my partner, various hospital personnel and the investigating detectives. She must now relive the abomination committed against her once more. Sue then moved to interview the arrestees; I'm not sure why, but she insisted on first talking to Paul. She once again advised Paul of his Miranda rights and then asked if he was willing to make a statement. Paul agreed to talk with Sue and remained just as cool as he had been since we made the arrest. Paul emphasized that he did not know Pam and had not seen her before this incident began. Paul stated, "I just thought I was gettin' a free shot of ass." After the interview with Paul concluded, Sue decided to interview Tom. At this point in time, Tom had become more than a little nervous. He was so sure that the discovery of the Glad sandwich bags was the necessary evidence to exonerate him and Paul; he couldn't imagine why he was still in custody. I decided to sit in on this interview. I had developed a bad feeling about the manner in which this investigation was proceeding.

Tom admitted knowing Pam, and that they had been friends for several years. He further admitted that they had never been involved in a romantic relationship at any time. Pam had visited Tom previously just to "kick it" as Tom described it. I asked Tom at what point did Pam develop a "crack" habit, and Tom stated he did know if she had a "crack" habit. I then asked if this was the first time she had bought "crack" from him, and Tom hesitated and then stated that it was the first time she had gotten "crack" from him. Sue asked a few more questions before I intervened: Do you always allow your customers to use the product before payment? Tom looked bewildered and then stated, "No, I don't do that." I went on to question why this time was so different, why Pam was allowed to use the product before payment. Tom failed to offer a logical answer to that line of questioning. Sue asked Tom about the baseball bat. Tom admitted having a baseball bat, and he then said he had the bat in his hand when he demanded sex as payment for the "crack" Pam smoked. He admitted standing in front of the door and blocking Pam's path to exit the apartment. He went on to say that he was holding the bat in his hand when he told Pam she had to consent to sex with him and Paul before she would be allowed. And he insisted that they did not rape Pam.

As I left that interview room, I was brimming with confidence that felony charges would be approved against Tom and Paul. The words, "If you use force or the threat of force" reverberated in my mind as I approached the front desk. Unwittingly, Tom had confessed to committing this crime, and he gave his buddy Paul up in the same breath. I cannot describe how totally befuddled I was when Sue informed us that she was NOT going to approve felony charges against Tom and Paul. I asked, "Were you not in the same room? Did you not hear that idiot confess to this?" Sue insisted she did not have enough evidence to approve the charges and worst, she failed to explain exactly what was lacking in our case. It was a little after 11:00 a.m. and I was angrier than I can describe. There is a fail-safe in these types of situations. I went to the watch commander's office and asked him to contact the street deputy so we could pursue an override. (In Chicago, a deputy superintendent of police is on the street to respond to major police actions and to respond to instances where watch commanders believe the Office of Felony Review has erred in refusing to assign felony charges in an arrest situation.) In response to my request for assistance from the street deputy, the watch commander looked at the clock and stated you guys have been four hours overtime on this, and it's time to wrap it up and get out of here. He instructed me to put misdemeanor charges on Tom and Paul and get off "his" clock.

An overwhelming feeling of dread came over me as I knew that I had to inform Pam the system had failed her. Pam had been violated once again, and in my opinion, this failure was the most heinous crime against her. This system, the vehicle with which she was supposed to attain justice, defiled her in a manner so egregious I struggled to find words to explain. It was MY job to deliver this message to Pam. And even though my partner and I worked as diligently as possible to attain justice for Pam, I knew that in her eyes, it could be me that represented the system that had violated her. This system violated her in a manner more devastating than Tom and Paul could ever. It is not the responsibility of Tom and Paul to protect and/or service her, it IS the responsibility of the system to provide such. Perhaps she could see in my eyes or hear in my voice how disappointed I was; maybe she could sense how difficult it was for me to deliver this message. She was devastated, but she did not lash out against me, she gave me a break. She did thank my partner and me for our efforts on her behalf. She told us that all she wanted to do at that moment was go home and shower. She wanted to see if she could wash away all the evil that had been done to her.

We, the detectives, my partner and I could not offer any logical reason why that in the eyes of this system she had not been the victim of a felony crime. I gave her the victim's copy of the police report and informed her of the court date for the misdemeanor charges against Tom and Paul. Pam was present in court for the misdemeanor charges against Tom and Paul. She sat through the morning's procedures, three hours, and was then informed her case was continued until the next month. Pam was present in court on that date, and once again after three hours, she was informed the case had been continued until the following month. On that date in March 1994, Pam failed to appear in court, and the charges against Tom and Paul were dismissed. The rape of Pam was now complete. Many times in my career, I was disappointed or angry when the complaining witness/victim failed to appear in court for proceedings against the offender. In this case, I was not disappointed, especially since I believed the biggest offender in this matter was the criminal justice system. I'll never know or understand why Sue denied the felony charges and why the watch commander believed it was more important to limit the overtime expenditure than to attain justice for Pam. Strictly as a matter of speculation, I believe the determining factors in this case were my victim was not well educated and poor, AND she was a woman.

Women have been marginalized in this country since its inception. Most of our criminal code originated from English Common Law. In English Common Law, it was legal for a man to beat his wife as long as the object utilized was no wider than the width of his thumb—"the rule of thumb." The state of Maryland adopted that law in the early 1600s. At one point, the women in America could not smoke in public. Women had to fight for decades to achieve the right to vote. "Keep 'em barefoot and pregnant" was a commonly accepted axiom in the country for centuries. The double standard regarding sexuality is firmly entrenched. Fathers expect their sons to go out and "sow their wild oats," but the daughter must remain a pristine virgin until marriage. If the son has multiple sexual conquests, Dad is proud and happy. However, if the daughter engages in the same promiscuity, she's a slut or tramp. Tragically, just as true has been the difficulty women have had being protected from unwanted sexual advances from men. There was a time in this country when women that reported being raped were first asked, "What were you wearing?" or "Why were you out at that time of night?" Questions like, "Did you lead him on?" were frequently asked of women complaining of rape. Since that time, "rape shield" laws have been passed seemingly with the intention of protecting women from this type of revictimization. But alas, there various sources that estimate anywhere between 80 to 88% of women who are sexually assaulted NEVER report the crime. I submit that is a caustic indictment against our criminal justice system and society as a whole. During the 2016 presidential campaign, a video of then "private citizen" Donald Trump was released that showed him bragging about the fact his celebrity allowed him to, without consent, grope women at his leisure (a crime in all fifty states). He attempted to explain the guttural language and his actions as just "locker room" talk. Christian Broadcasting Network founder Pat Robertson defended this as just "macho" talk. Perhaps we should expect more from a "man of the cloth." And although the video of Donald Trump is eleven years old should we not view it as insight to his "actual" feelings about women? The double standard extends into interpersonal relationships as well. There are men that strongly believe it is quite permissible, even natural that they pursue sexual conquests outside their committed relationships, but IF his wife or girlfriend were to do the same, OH MY, that would be the most unforgiveable sin. "It's in a man's nature to continually pursue other conquests." "Boys will be boys." These and a slew of other clichés have long been standards in our society.

It is my contention that our society fails to consistently acknowledge the horror, the extreme violation and injury of rape. Far too often, victims of this heinous crime are met with indifference and dismissal. There are far too many occurrences when a severely traumatized person is met with a cavalier attitude and empty response. This is completely and totally unacceptable. Examples of this callous attitude have been displayed by elected officials. Abortion rights have been one of the hottest political footballs in this country for decades. Of course, unwanted pregnancies that can occur as a result of this heinous violation are part of the debate. One abortion opponent, Congressman Trent Franks offered the moronic argument that it was not possible for the victim of a rape to be impregnated. (How did that person make it out of high school biology? Who did you pay and how much did it cost?) Judge James Leon Holmes offers: "Concern for rape victims is a red herring because conception from rape occurs with the same frequency as snow fall in Miami." Various studies report that better than thirty-two thousand pregnancies result from rape each year. Former presidential candidate Rick Santorum stated, "Raped women should accept the gift of life." The Speaker of the House, Paul Ryan stated: "The method of conception doesn't change the definition of life." Congressman Lawrence Lockman of Maine stated: "If a woman can have an abortion, why can't a man use his superior size and strength to force himself on a woman?" (He later apologized for this nonsensical statement.) I invite Mr. Ryan, Mr. Santorum and others who share this view to consult with a woman IMMEDIATELY after she has been violated and promote their view of how she should feel about mothering the child of her assailant. This is the most horrendous violation any person can experience. Misters Santorum and Ryan purport themselves as individuals qualified to make the decision about how the victim should feel, react and view the consequences of the sin committed against them. I believe the creation of life should be an act of love and not a violent, horrendous invasion. I invite them to step down from their bully pulpits and seek to connect with the victims. Counsel a woman in the immediate aftermath of the worst experience of her life and see how receptive she'll be to the direction you seek to offer. Not every victim will seek to terminate a pregnancy caused by rape. However, in some cases, the victim is raped again and again by our court system. In 2009, Jaime Melendez raped a fourteen-year-old girl and impregnated her during the crime. Mr. Melendez was sentenced to probation for his crime. (I shall address this later in the chapter.) Melendez was ordered to pay child support to his victim. In an effort to avoid paying child support, Melendez initiated a civil effort to gain visitation rights for the child. He of course offered to drop the proceedings IF he was excused of any financial responsibility for the child. Shauna Prewitt has spent two years in court fighting her rapist for custody of the child produced by that rape.

I suggest, no implore, the elected officials that want to eliminate abortion as an option for the woman who has been raped to craft legislation that will protect the victims of rape from these heartless and cruel exercises. Failing to do such demonstrates callous short-sightedness on the part of those who purport themselves "defenders of all human life." Stop for a moment and envision the conversation between the rape victim and the child conceived by the rape. How does the mother explain to her child that he/she must spend the weekend with the man who violated her? What message are we sending? I call upon the foes of abortion to demonstrate that you loathe these offenders, and that you have compassion for the victims. Enact legislation to ensure the victims of rape never have to answer petitions for visitation or custody of the children they criminally and cruelly fathered. During the course of this text, I have not identified any state politicians, and I recognize this movement would have to begin statewide. However, I do believe that federally elected officials can lead the way, they can initiate the conversation. This issue transcends party affiliation and/or one's views on abortion. It is strictly about fairness and decency. It concerns demonstrating appropriate sensitivity to victims of this heinous crime.

In general, our society has continuously failed to adequately address the viscous and horrible crime of rape. For reasons that I cannot comprehend, our Criminal Justice System consistently fails victims of rape. One glaring example of such is the inexplicable failure to process rape kits in this country. It is reported that over FOUR HUNDRED THOUSAND rape kits in this nation have not been processed. Many of which are from crimes that occurred so long ago that the statute of limitations has expired. I'm going to take a brief detour at this point.

It is my contention that there is no credible reason for a statute of limitations to exist in cases of felonious crimes against persons. And by that, I am speaking of violent acts committed against another human being. The stated purpose for the necessity of a statute of limitations is to ensure convictions occur only on evidence (physical or eyewitness) that has not deteriorated over time. The argument is the state should be limited in its opportunity to prosecute people for alleged crimes they may or may not have committed. Many legal experts believe the longer it takes to bring a matter to trial, the less reliable the evidence will be. And I certainly understand that could very well present a challenge. However, with the advent of certain technological advances, there is the possibility empirical, physical evidence can be preserved in such manner as to be just as viable when it was collected as it will be when the offender is arrested. Let us not forget there is no statute of limitations for murder, and the burden of proof for ANY offense does not deviate. Guilt beyond a reasonable doubt shall always be the standard; the passage of time should not excuse the offender from the consequences of his/her deeds. My view is that the statute of limitations awards criminals for being lucky or skillful enough to avoid detection. At present, our Criminal Justice System affords offenders the opportunity to eschew responsibility for the heinous acts they've committed. The primary purpose of our Criminal Justice System is to provide a vehicle by which victims can attain justice for crimes committed against them in a civil manner. Vigilantism has no place in a civilized society. However, the existence of a statute of limitations for horrible acts committed against persons can encourage a person to "take the law into their hands." I believe that our Criminal Justice System should send the message that no matter how long it takes, it shall tirelessly work to provide justice for the victims of violent crimes.

And now back to the shameful effort our system continues to make regarding addressing the brutal crime of rape. The federal government, each state and each county within each state has a chief law enforcement official. At the state and county levels, those individuals are elected by "we the people." The Attorney General of the United States is nominated by the president and confirmed by our Congress. The aforementioned four hundred thousand untested rape kits have accumulated over the course of decades. During which time, these erstwhile public servants have done nothing to address this matter. In fact, I've not discovered any evidence that any of them attempted to make this an issue. Furthermore, those persons that have challenged incumbent prosecutors in the various elections have failed to address this matter in any discernable manner. The inane statute of limitations has completely devalued many of these untested rape kits, and what's most tragic is the fact that the victims have been failed miserably. The victims have been violated by both the offender and the system that has the responsibility for protecting and serving them. More than likely the water weak excuse these officials will offer is that they lack the resources, the funding to process each of these kits. They may offer that each of the kits associated with an arrest were processed. And perhaps in their eyes, that is sufficient. That rationale ignores the fact that a processed rape kit may provide investigating detectives with evidence to advance the investigation of the crime. Perhaps, the investigating detectives will garner evidence sufficient to make an arrest. We can't know what may result from responsibly processing these kits within a reasonable period of time. This cavalier attitude helps explain why, depending upon the source, an estimated 60 to 88% of women that are sexually assaulted in this country never report the crime. I submit that is a caustic indictment against our Criminal Justice System. Unless you were a test-tube baby, there has been at least ONE significant woman in your life. We must demand that our elected officials work diligently and effectively to remedy this inexcusable crisis.

As previously illustrated in the rape of Pam, women cannot be assured they shall attain justice even after their assailants are arrested. Armed with the discretion, certain laws allow judges can mete out the most ridiculous sentences a person can imagine. One time, Supreme Court nominee Robert Bork stated that there were for too many justices that legislated from the bench as opposed to enforcing the law as it is written. On March 24, 2016, a judge in Tulsa, OK determined that a seventeen-year-old boy was not guilty of the forcible sodomy of a sixteen-year-old girl because her alcoholic beverage consumption left her unconscious. "Forcible sodomy cannot occur where a victim is so intoxicated as to be completely unconscious at the time of the sexual act of oral copulation." Help me understand. CONSENT! Regardless of the state each law written regarding sex crimes addresses the issue of consent. Sixteen year olds CANNOT consent. An unconscious person CANNOT consent. This judge's ruling is consistent with the archaic "victim blaming" mind-set that rape shield laws were supposed to vitiate. The sixteen-year-old girl should not have been consuming alcoholic beverages, and she most assuredly should not have drunk herself unconscious. But do we want to send the message that if/when a person causes themselves to become unconscious by whatever means, they are no longer protected by the laws of the land? In my opinion, this judge sent a message that when this young lady engaged in this binge drinking she surrendered her right of protection from unwanted or unsolicited sexual advances from others. I believe that the judge was scolding the young lady about her reckless behavior and telling her that such behavior affords cads like this seventeen year old the license to violate her. Enforcing the law was not the primary objective of this judge: teaching the girl a lesson was this judge's mission.

"Prison might be too tough on him." Judge Aaron Persky stated. Brock Turner was convicted of sexual assault in the State of California; he was facing a potential fourteen years in prison. Turner sexually assaulted a woman while she was drugged and incapacitated. When the sentencing portion of this legal procedure occurred, Judge Persky sentenced Turner to SIX months in prison. His rationale was that a longer term in prison would be too harsh for this defendant. Wow, too harsh for the convicted rapist! After the verdict, the victim published her heartfelt impressions of this sordid affair. As I read her words, I thought of each of the rape victims with whom I interacted during my career. I thought of Sue and the feelings she expressed when I had to share with her the misguided decision of the assistant state's attorney who handled her case. This victim's expression mirrored every bit of disappointment and betrayal as Sue's. In no uncertain terms, she lets it be known that the unkindest injury of this ordeal was delivered by system that is charged with the responsibility of protecting her. Judge Persky's sentencing withstood judicial review. I'm sure the argument is that a panel of jurists is far better equipped to evaluate the performance of a judge than laypersons. As a former police officer, I understand that there are some actions taken by police officers that are better understood by people who "do the job" than by those who have never been police officers. However, fecal matter is fecal matter regardless of how it is packaged, dressed or perfumed. This case provides an overwhelmingly obvious example of why it is critically important that voters become especially more educated about the job performance of the judges for which we vote.

My Christian faith prohibits me from feeling this way, but perhaps if more of our "decision makers" personally experienced the horror of this vile offense, they would have greater sensitivity to this matter. If the experience was up close and personal, perhaps addressing this would garner a greater sense of urgency. Nancy Reagan was staunchly against stem cell research until husband Ron developed Alzheimer's. In 1985, ABC produced a made-for-television movie, *The Rape of Richard Beck*, directed by Karen Arthur and written by James Hirsch. It featured Richard Crenna in an Emmy Award winning role as a cynical police detective. Detective Richard Beck was of the opinion that victims of rape had a degree of culpability, fault for the offense committed against them. And then one dark night, Detective Beck became the victim of a sexual assault; he was raped. His tragic experience provided an acutely different perspective. The basic humanity we each should possess should not require we experience a heinous wrong to appreciate the gravity of that crime. If we fail to demand that our public servants address these matters with the sensitivity they deserve, we are just as guilty as the perpetrators of these horrific acts.

The relentless pursuit of the pagan god...money all too often colors the decisions made by persons in positions of responsibility. Major college athletics is one of the most lucrative businesses in this nation. The chief revenue sports of college athletics are football and basketball. At seven million dollars a year, Nick Saban, the head football coach for the University of Alabama, is the highest paid state employee in Alabama. During Coach Saban's seven-year tour, his teams have won four national championships and are perennially ranked among the top two or three teams in the nation. His contribution to this institution of higher education is measured strictly in the revenue the football program generates for the school. This is not unique to Coach Saban's program or the University of Alabama. During my senior year at the University of Illinois at Chicago, I served as the student representative to the Board of Trustees for the University of Illinois. It was during that year that I learned firsthand that the business of an institute for higher education was BUSINESS. Most decisions made by the board revolved around the economic benefit to the university—all four campuses. I believe that the business of higher education explains why Baylor University responded so irresponsibly to the litany of reported sexual assaults by members of its football team. It is reported that during the presidency of Kenneth Starr, there may have been as many as fifty-two rapes in four years. There is active litigation in federal court to this effect. Kenneth Starr, who one may remember spent a ton of our tax dollars in an effort to prove that then President Bill Clinton was cheating on his wife, managed an administration that reportedly turned a deaf ear to dozens of complaints regarding this matter. The lawsuit further alleges the football program utilized sex to earn commitments from blue-chip football recruits. It appears the focus of Kenneth Starr's administration was to use whatever means they could envision to establish and maintain a first-rate football program. The dignity, safety and security of the female students were a distant second to their goal of establishing such.

A National Collegiate Athletic Association (NCAA) investigation of the basketball program at Louisville University has revealed the utilization of strippers and prostitutes may have been a tool for recruitment. John Barr of ESPN reported that one time assistant basketball coach Andre McGee routinely provided money to hire strippers and prostitutes for blue-chip basketball prospects. In an interview with the possible "Madame," Katina Powell, she stated she received money to provide the strippers and was informed the strippers could earn extra cash for sexual favors if they so desired. The basketball program at Louisville University has been a consistent source of major revenue for that university. As previously stated, basketball and football are chief revenue providers for colleges and universities across this nation. My experience as a member of the Board of Trustees for the University of Illinois taught me that meaningful intentions and goodwill do not provide the requisite revenue to provide a quality education. However, dehumanizing women in the manner in which I've just described is inexcusable. They should not be offered as sacrificial lambs to satisfy brutish, amoral thugs. They should not be bullion or prizes offered to entice student athletes to choose one school over others for enrollment. This type of behavior is a shameful part of the tapestry of indifference for crimes committed against our women.

False reports of rape and/or sexual assault work as a disservice to the multitude of actual victims. It is inexcusably self-centered and horribly wrong. These selfish acts provide fodder for those individuals who downplay the trauma of this beastly act.

With regards to the issue of false accusations of sexual assault, one case that I personally handled stands out for me. I responded to a call concerning a rape that had just occurred. The complainant met me on the sidewalk in front of the single-family home where this sexual assault reportedly took place. She was obviously distraught; crying hysterically with her clothing disheveled and hair all over her head. While I was attempting to interview her, a young man emerged from the home at which we were standing. He approached us and asked what was happening. The complainant immediately began screaming, "That's him, that's him, he raped me, and he raped me."

The young man recoiled, threw his hands into the air and replied, "I don't know what you talkin' 'bout." At that time, a few backup units arrived on the scene, and we handcuffed the young man as he continued to protest. After placing him into the back of my squad car, we spoke with the complainant once more. She stated this young man was her friend, but that they were not romantically involved. In fact, she informed us that he was married, and that she knew the young man's wife. One of the female officers on the scene transported the victim to the hospital for the rape kit, and I transported the young man to the police station for processing. The young man continued to protest his arrest stating that he did have consensual sex with the young lady. He stated that he could prove the sex was consensual if I made a telephone call to his friend. The address of this alleged sexual assault was less than one block from the police station, and the young man did not resist any part of the arrest. I escorted him into the station and took him to one of the interview rooms. After reading the Miranda warning to him, I asked if he wanted to talk about this incident in any way. Once again, he assured me that if I called his friend, the friend could provide evidence that the sex he had with the complainant was consensual. After thinking about it a little more seriously, I opted to take the number from the young man and call his friend. I was very surprised that the friend arrived at the police station in less than twenty minutes with a video cassette. The friend assured me that this video cassette would exonerate my arrestee. The contents of the video cassette displayed the complainant on her knees performing an act of fellatio on the arrestee. The complainant looked into the camera during the filming and waved. After which, she focused her attention on her craft. I immediately went into the interview room and removed the handcuffs from my actual victim. When the young lady arrived at the station from the hospital, I invited her into the interview room. When she entered the room, I applied the handcuffs to her wrist and informed her that she was being charged with filing a false official report. She was stunned. Of course, she protested and asked why she was being arrested after being raped. I was able to silence her protests by informing her that I had viewed the videotape. Of course, I inventoried the tape as evidence against her for purposes of a trial should she choose to pursue such.

One of the things that troubled me about this situation and situations like this is that the offense for which I arrested this young lady is a misdemeanor. However, the real victim in this case, the accused young man was facing class X felony charges. We've all heard of men that have been falsely accused and convicted of rape; after which they've spent significant years of their lives in prison. Later, the alleged victim recants, or other evidence surfaces that exonerates them. Time is something that cannot be repaid. There is absolutely no making up for time lost. Not one of us is guaranteed the next breath; hence, we have absolutely no time to lose. Given that fact I believe that when a person(s) intentionally falsely accuses another of a crime and that person serves time in prison, the person(s) that made the false accusation should spend just as much time incarcerated as the falsely imprisoned person. Furthermore, in a case such as the one I handled where the intentionally false accusation was made and further investigation revealed said accusation is false, the person making the intentionally false accusation should be charged with an offense equal to falsely charged offense. In the case I handled, I believe the complainant should have been charged with a class X felony; she sought to ruin that young man's life with this heinous charge. Therefore, she should have faced a charge equal to her intentionally false accusation. Toying with another person's life in such manner is reprehensible and should be addressed accordingly.

It is reported that anywhere between 80 to 88% of women in this nation that are sexually assaulted do not report the offense. That is a staggering number and a caustic indictment of our Criminal Justice System and society as a whole. One could advance the argument that enacting a law that will lead to the prosecution and imprisonment of a woman for falsely accusing a man of rape will further dissuade women from reporting this offense. However, my suggestion involves INTENTIONALLY accusing a person of an offense for which the complainant KNOWS that person is not guilty. The key element of the offense is there must be intent on the part of the offender to bring false charges against another.

Additionally, I believe that it is necessary to relieve the judiciary of much of its discretion regarding sentencing offenders found guilty of rape. The fact that persons of varied socioeconomic backgrounds are sentenced differently is an affront to the essence of justice. When a judge expresses more concern for the well-being of the offender than the victim in a case of sexual assault, it is BGO (blinding glimpse of the obvious) that this system is broken. I propose the mandatory minimum a person should serve for sexual assault/rape is twenty-five years if there is no weapon involved, thirty-five years when a weapon is involved. We must send the message to victims of this horrific crime that our society will no longer mete out inconsistent justice in these matters. The location (state), socioeconomic status of victim and/or offender is inconsequential in these matters. The consequences for this heinous act should be just as decisively harsh as the offense. Given this nation's history of inconsistency when dealing with this offense earning the trust of victims of this offense will be a long, arduous journey; but this is a journey upon which we should embark immediately, if not sooner.

CHILD SEX ABUSE

My personal belief is that a child is the most precious gift with which the Lord can bless a person. I am unabashedly an all-day sucker for children. We each of us are familiar with phrases like "the children are our future" and "it takes a village to raise a child." I am quite confident that an overwhelming majority of people in our nation will agree that our children are precious commodities that should be treasured, nurtured and protected at all costs. However, I submit that with regard to child sex abuse, the protection that we provide is woefully inadequate. There are far too many cases where convicted child sex offenders reoffend. Profit margin, revenue generated, etc., has colored the decision making in cases involving mass child sex abuse and/or exploitation. And in some cases, inexcusable cowardice has some complicit in this, perhaps the most heinous crime existent in humanity. Yes, I really mean the most heinous crime a person can commit. One might, maybe be able to name something just as horrible as this crime; but I CHALLENGE anyone to identify something more foul than sexually abusing a child. I am not in court, under oath, offering unbiased testimony in a trial, so I will NOT attempt to conceal the utter disdain I have for those persons that sexually abuse children. During my career in the Chicago Police Department, I had to exercise discipline while dealing with cases of child sex abuse. I am going to share with you the most memorable of those cases.

In the summer of 1999, I was on patrol at approximately 12:30 in the afternoon. While driving down one of the side streets on my beat, my attention was drawn to a woman waving her arms in an effort to have me stop. This woman was in the company of another woman and a small child—a girl. I pulled over to the curb to learn what I could do to assist the woman waving at me. I noticed that the other woman was more than a wee bit unkempt. She reeked of alcoholic beverage, and she had what we officers termed the PHD (pumpkin head deluxe). The woman that flagged me down informed me that she, the little girl, had something to tell me. I looked down at this darling little girl who appeared withdrawn and very uneasy. At this point, I did not know the dynamics of this situation. I asked the spokeswoman how she was related to the child, and she informed me that she was a friend of the mother, the drunken woman with the multiple contusions, and the little girl was the daughter of drunken woman. I wasn't sure what to expect, but I decided it would be advantageous to separate the child from the adult women as much as possible without making the child too uncomfortable. I began preliminary conversation with the child in an effort to earn some trust.

After we conversed for a few minutes, I asked her if there was something that she wanted me to know. She nodded her head yes, and I assured her that she could tell me anything; I let her know that it was my job to help her, and that I was anxious to help her in any way I could. At that point, she said to me, "My daddy touched me." That was something for which I was not prepared. I maintained composure and asked her where her daddy touched her. The darling child pointed between her legs. That's when a sick, sinking feeling came over me. Maintain, maintain is what I kept telling myself. I have to get this story straight if I'm going to be able to help this baby in any way. I then asked how did her daddy touch her, and she replied, "He licked me." I know that children can be coached and used as pawns in disputes between adults. Given that reality, I continued the conversation with this little angel. I asked her the same questions in a variety of ways, and the story remained the same. At that point, I was convinced that this baby had been violated. I have written how important it is to divorce one's self from the emotion; how one should not allow emotion to dictate one's actions. I have prided myself in my ability to live by that creed…mostly. But in this situation, I found myself cheating the creed. You see at the time I was talking with this baby, I could not help but think about my own baby. That child was four and my child was four. When I looked at that baby, I could not help but think about my baby. I was able to maintain my composure in the presence of the child, her drunken mother and the family friend. I radioed for an assist as I knew the child had to go to the hospital. The family friend was able to tell me where I could find this little girl's father. I wanted to MEET this guy. I wanted for him and me to spend some "quality time alone." After the assist unit drove away with the child, her mother and family friend, I radioed the dispatcher to inform her where I was going, and that I would be making an arrest when I arrived. I did NOT ask for an assist unit as I did not want to draw any of my co-workers into a potentially bad situation.

When I arrived at the apartment building, Officer James Booker was awaiting my arrival. I told him that I could handle this, and that he didn't need to be there. He responded that he did not come to assist me, but he was there to ensure that I did not lose my job. We proceeded into the apartment complex, and I found the culprit exactly where the family friend said I'd find him. Sadly, he did not resist arrest, and I took him into custody without incident. I drove him to the district station for processing, and of course, he continuously denied culpability for this heinous act. After we arrived in the district station, I had to notify the Special Victims Unit and then the State Department of Children and Family Services (DCFS). The detective in SVU with whom I spoke informed me that the child would have to be taken to La Rabida Hospital for a "victim sensitive interview" before we could pursue charges against the father. I asked at what point that would occur, and he told me he could not give me a definite answer. Oh, so in the meantime, am I supposed to send this child back home with him? I asked the detective to say that aloud and see how it sounded to him. At that point, I realized that there was a strong possibility this baby would have to go back home with this person. The prospect of such was completely unacceptable to me, so I telephoned DCFS and shared the information I had. I impressed upon the urgency of the matter and implored them to come to our station and take protective custody of this child. They agreed and informed me that an agent was on route.

While awaiting the arrival of the young girl, I researched police calls to her home address. The mother mentioned that she had called the police the night prior, so I began research of police reports generated for that address. I came to learn that at least five reports for domestic battery had been generated at that address over the past four weeks. After reading the reports, I discovered the mother had called the police to report being beaten by the father. When the police arrived, he had fled the area. She was advised to go to domestic violence court and secure an order of protection and court summons on each occasion. Furthermore, it was explained that when he returned, she could call the police and have him arrested on the report that had been generated. When the mother, child and family friend arrived at the station, I pulled the mother aside and asked her to share with me what happened that she had to call the police five times to report being beaten by her husband. What she told me turned my stomach. Each beating took place after she discovered her husband sexually assaulting their daughter. She found him performing oral sex on their daughter and challenged him concerning the matter. However, she failed to report to the responding officers or any other authorities what her husband was doing to their daughter. Each report generated for that address was for a domestic battery and nothing more. Parents and legal guardians are compelled by law to report any and all instances of abuse to a child. Based upon that fact, I took her into custody and filed the appropriate charges against her. Armed with the five reports for domestic battery, I appropriately charged the father. Representatives from DCFS arrived at the police station and took protective custody of the little girl. DCFS notified her maternal grandmother who came to their office that evening: the grandmother was awarded temporary custody. The father was never officially charged with any offense concerning his daughter. But oddly and inexplicably, the mother was found guilty (by plea bargain) of knowing of the abuse and failing to report it. As for the little girl, approximately five weeks later, I was notified to appear in juvenile court for a hearing initiated by DCFS. The State Department of Children and Family Services summoned both parents to this hearing for the purpose of terminating their respective parental authority. I answered my subpoena on that date and time: reported to the court sergeant's office, signed in and then went to the appropriate courtroom.

What happened next I will remember when I have Alzheimer's and amnesia. As I entered the courtroom, the child, that baby, ran to me and solidly embraced my left leg. She then said to me, "Thank you, thank you for keeping him away from me." I stood there trembling like a leaf on a tree, and I don't really remember how I responded. The flood of emotion that rushed through me is indescribable. Of course, this child did not fully understand what her father was doing to her, but she knew it was wrong. She knew that it made her uncomfortable, and she was desperate for it to stop. Her mother failed to do what was necessary to protect her, and there was only so much the friend of the family could do. I felt honored that there was an opportunity for me to play a part in the action necessary to rescue this precious child from the undeserving individuals who produced her. "Hell, you need a license to buy a dog or drive a car. Hell, you need a license to catch a fish. But any butt-reaming asshole can be a father" (Keanu Reeves, motion picture *Parenthood,* produced by Amblin Entertainment, directed by Ron Howard, written by Lowell Ganz and Babaloo Mandel, 1989). As I stood there in that baby's embrace, I know that if someone had approached me and blew on me, I would have fallen to the floor. The grandmother approached me to thank me for what I had done, and I remember handing my business card to her. I implored her to call me any time of day or night if she smelled that father in the vicinity. I assured her that if he attempted to make contact with her or the child that I would decisively handle that situation. The father failed to appear; the mother entered the courtroom forty minutes late and in her usual drunken state. The judge formally terminated the parental rights of the birth parents and awarded full and permanent custody to the maternal grandmother. When possible, I stopped by the residence and checked on the child and grandmother. The grandmother assured that there was no attempt by the father to contact the child.

I did not personally handle this next case, but I was present in the police interview room when a forty-year-old man was brought in for sodomizing his then thirteen-year-old nephew. This abuse had been an ongoing event for seven years. It came to light when one of his younger sisters called the police after she found her thirteen-year-old nephew sodomizing her six-year-old son. Picture if you will a two-flat apartment building where all the residents are family members. On the first floor, the elder sister, her husband, and three children resided. The younger sister and her six-year-old son lived on the second floor. The adults in the building have been instrumental parts of the lives of each child. On one Saturday afternoon, the younger sister had a few errands to run, so she asked her thirteen-year-old nephew to come upstairs and sit with his six-year-old cousin while she was out. She finished somewhat sooner than expected and returned home to a horrifying situation. She came home to her thirteen-year-old nephew sodomizing her six-year-old son. The potpourri of emotions that ensured overcame her. She was so beside herself. How could this be? The nephew she loved just like a son was defiling her son in the most despicable manner possible. Her family members advised her to refrain from alerting the police and allow the family, with the assistance of their pastor, to handle this matter. After thinking it over, she decided her best course of action was to call the police. She wanted to ensure that both boys received the help they desperately needed.

When the police arrived on the scene, she reported what she discovered. The reaction of the responding officers was something the family members had not yet considered. The officers were curious to learn "who" had victimized the thirteen-year-old boy. Their attitude was that this boy did not read a book or see a movie that inspired this action. This boy has been a victim, and he is just acting out something that was forced upon him. Further investigation revealed that for the past seven years, the thirteen year old had been the victim of his forty-year-old ex-con uncle. Most child rapists ARE persons close to the family, someone that has established trust in one way or another. The stereotypical "Chester the Molester" monster is the exception to the rule. Most child molesters earn the trust of the primary caregivers of their victims. Establishing trust is a critical component in their nefarious scheme. This uncle ruined the lives of two boys, and in the dark recesses of his mind, he has done nothing wrong. He understands his actions are illegal, but he rationalized it in such manner as to give himself permission to carry out his dastardly deeds. The six-year-old nephew is just collateral damage, or perhaps he was the intended next target. Essentially, this uncle ruined the lives of two innocent young children, and they just happened to be members of HIS family.

Earlier in this chapter, we considered the multitude of rape allegations involving the football program at Baylor University. Let us now examine the child sex abuse scandal with the football program at Penn State University. Tragically, this scandal culminated the career of legendary head football coach Joe Paterno or "Joe Pa" as he was affectionately known. Even more tragic, however, is the indelible damage done to ten young children reportedly victimized by Assistant Coach Jerry Sandusky. In 2012, Jerry Sandusky was convicted on forty-five counts of sexually abusing children at the football camps he operated on the campus of Penn State University. And once again, it appears there was much more concern about the potential ill effects on the football program than the well-being of the children whose innocence had been stolen. In addition to the conviction of Sandusky, former high-ranking administrators from Penn State are on trial for their respective roles in the cover up of this atrocity. Graham Spanier, president; Tim Curley, athletic director; Gary Schultz, vice-president. These individuals, supposed stewards of the well-being of all who utilized the facilities of Penn State University appear to have turned a blind eye to the depravity of this convicted child sex offender. And I'm quite sure their ONLY motivation was to protect the "cash cow" that is the football program at Penn State University. This motley mess came to light after Assistant Coach Mike McQueary reported an incident he reportedly observed in the men's locker room to Head Coach Joe Paterno. McQueary informed Paterno that on the previous day, he observed Sandusky sodomizing a ten-year-old boy in the shower. Okay, let's pause right here. This fully adult male reportedly witnessed an adult violating a child, AND as a result, he decided to inform the boss of this heinous act…THE NEXT DAY! Well, not exactly. It is reported that McQueary's IMMEDIATE action was to leave the area and telephone his own father. Supposedly, during this conversation, he told his father what he had witnessed and asked his advice on a course of action. In the meantime, this child is being violently assaulted by an adult. WOW! I do not purport to speak for anyone other than myself, but I absolutely know that IF I had telephoned my father with that story, his response would have been WHAT? WHAT DID YOU SAY? Okay, boy where are you? I'll come to you and show you what you should do. Without a doubt, I KNOW what I would have done had I witnessed this heinous act. I can make that declaration based upon what I have DONE!

During the summer of 1988, I was informed by four young girls, ages six thru ten, that a man was in the alley exposing his genitals to them. Of course, I had to investigate; and when I found this individual at the mouth of the alley with his hand stuck down his pants, he and I spent some "quality time alone" in that alley. At the conclusion of this session, I impressed upon him that it would be in his best interest if I never again saw him in my neighborhood. The last thing I said to him was that he had ten seconds to get out of my face, and that eight of those seconds were gone! He abided by my edict, left hurriedly, and I never again saw that individual. I committed a crime that day; I violated the law and committed the offense of battery (Illinois law). My emotions played a significant part in my decision making regarding this matter, although my knowledge of the Criminal Justice System played some part in what I did. I cannot, will not advocate vigilantism as an appropriate response to any crime regardless of how heinous the act. I had no legal right to "beat the brakes off" that person, and I will not attempt to justify such. However, it is my assertion that "we" impress upon our lawmakers how critically important it is that the consequences for these acts become DECIDELY harsher. It has been later revealed that McQueary was reportedly the victim of child sex abuse. That is a horrible and tragic reality. However, I submit it is not an excuse for failing to take more decisive and IMMEDIATE action for the heinous act he reportedly witnessed. He did not have to physically involve himself (although without hesitation, I would have). He could have shouted something, made some noise, done something to alert Sandusky that he was being observed. And he most assuredly should have CALLED THE POLICE! That child deserved BETTER, and as a previous victim, he should have known such. I categorically reject the notion that he needed to call his father to ask for instructions. He failed that child MISERABLY! It is my assertion that his failure to act is equivocal to the alleged cover-up actions of Spanier, Culley, and Schultz.

Albert Lord, a member of the Board of Trustees of Penn State University, has been quoted as saying that he has begun to run out of sympathy for the thirty-five-year-old "so-called victims" with seven-digit net worth. Perhaps Mr. Lord is so obtuse that he believes income and age can provide solace for the victims of child sex abuse. Or maybe as a member of the board, his primary motivation is protecting the "bottom line" for the university and continued conversation about the egregious crimes committed on that campus threatens future revenue generation. Whatever his motivation, heartless declarations like that are better kept to one's self—this statement should never have been made publicly.

I completed twelve years of studies in the Catholic School System of Chicago. During that time, I never had a criminal incident with any of the staff or clergy. I knew many other people in Catholic Schools, boys and girls, and I am completely unaware of any instances of inappropriate behavior by the faculty and/or staff of the Catholic School System. My daughter was a student in the Catholic School System. I was baptized and confirmed in the Catholic Church, and I am currently a practicing Catholic. However, I recognize the difference between Catholicism and the Catholic Church. The 2015 Academy Award winning movie *Spotlight*, directed by Tom McCarthy and written by Josh Singer & Tom McCarthy, tells the true story of an investigation led by the Boston Globe that uncovered the horrible reality of pedophile priests in the City of Boston. "Spotlight" was the name given the investigative section of the Boston Globe and what it uncovered shook the foundation of the Catholic Church. The instances of cover up and misdirection reverberated from Boston to the Vatican in Rome. *Spotlight* details how the Catholic Church systematically covered the countless instances of sexual misconduct involving a multitude of clergy, priests in particular. The sacrament of Confession is one of the Canons of Catholicism; it is one of the Seven Sacraments. However, what became clear is that the Catholic Church entertained confessions by offending clergy and then moved the offenders to different parishes where they reoffended. This shell game became a common practice; the ultimate goal of which was to protect the assets of the church. There is nothing in the tenants of Catholicism that fosters or promotes sexually abusing children. The vow of chastity taken by clergy members does not provide allowance for sexual misconduct of any type. It appears as though the problem may be as certain clergy ascend the ranks their focus becomes the fiduciary responsibility of their respective office as opposed to saving souls and spreading the Word of the Lord. Seemingly, they forget their responsibility to the parishioners they serve. There is no rational explanation for addressing an offense as serious as sexually abusing a child by relocating the offender to another parish. That is of course if the primary focus is protecting the children: if the decision makers recognize the pedophile will take his/her proclivities with them to whatever location. The fact these heinous acts were committed against countless children and the response from church officials was so negligent is completely inexcusable. Catholic Church officials had a moral duty to prioritize the children over the "business" of the church. The failure to protect the children of the church is polar opposite of what Catholicism teaches. The church officials who engaged in this practice are just as guilty as the pedophiles they protected; in fact, their sin is even more heinous. It has been demonstrated that the pedophile cannot exercise control over this proclivity; the bureaucrat's failure to act was the result of forethought. It is my belief these decisions were made simply to protect the image of the Catholic Church and its vast financial resources. There can be no greater shame than sacrificing children for a cause so shallow. It is important to note that the individuals responsible for these crimes are relatively few in number. The majority of the clergy and staff of the Catholic Church work diligently and honorably to serve its parishioners.

In 2014, Springfield, MO, Joseph Presley was convicted of twice molesting the eight-year-old boy left in his charge; he was supposed to be the babysitter. Judge Calvin Holden meted out a ten-year SUSPENDED sentence for this atrocity. What's worse is that he suspended the sentence and ordered Presley to serve a thirty-day "shock" sentence. I submit the only SHOCK in this exercise is that Presley spent but thirty days in jail for an offense that heinous. Presley violated a sacred trust and devastated a young life with an evil, despicable act, and for that, his penalty is thirty days of imprisonment and a lifelong requirement for sex offender registry. The Eighth Amendment protects us against cruel and unusual punishment; but the criminal code should protect us from the nefarious acts of evil doers. Presley spent THIRTY days in jail for devastating this young person. Others have spent three, five, twenty, or more years of incarceration for the same violation. There is no consistency regarding this matter. As I've previously stated, one may be able to name something just as heinous as sexually abusing a child, but I challenge anyone to identify something worse. IF we are going to make a sincere effort to protect our children from this type of debauchery, the punishment MUST be hard and fast: it MUST be consistent. Determinate sentencing HAS TO BE part of the methodology utilized in our quest to protect our children. Members of the judiciary have demonstrated beguiling inconsistency in sentencing. Coupled with the statute of limitations, TRUE justice for and protection of our children is seriously hampered.

The former Speaker of the House, Dennis Hastert, described as a serial child molester, was sentenced to fifteen years in prison for misappropriating campaign funds to cover up his crimes. Of course, the statute of limitations for those crimes had expired. He successfully bought his way out of prosecution for committing a series of horrific crimes. This has to be intolerable; we must work to ensure this can never again occur. With regard to sentencing, I propose that if the offender is eighteen years of age or more and the victim is twelve years of age or less, the DETERMINATE sentence be life, without the possibility of parole; the offender should never again breathe free air. If the offender is eighteen years of age or more and the victim is thirteen to seventeen years of age, the DETERMINATE sentence be a MINIMUM of thirty years. Any person eighteen years or more found guilty of the participation of producing or distributing child pornography should receive a DETERMINATE sentence of life, without the possibility of parole. Persons under the age of eighteen found guilty of the same should be sentenced to a minimum of thirty years of incarceration. The punishment MUST/SHOULD fit the crime! We must no longer offer mere "lip service" when we proclaim our commitment to protecting our children from these unspeakable acts. Furthermore, any person age eighteen or older found guilty of trafficking children of any age for any reason should be given a DETERMINATE sentence of life, without the possibility of parole.

In the Presley case, it is reported that since he was a member of a church that he would receive sufficient counseling through that church, and the said counseling will ensure that he never again violate a child in such manner. How'd that work out with the pedophile priests? It is not my intention to summarily dismiss the notion that "some" child sex offenders can be redeemed. And I am fully aware of how harsh life, without the possibility of parole is. It is my assertion that releasing someone convicted of this offense puts other children at risk, and that is an unacceptable risk. I am equally aware of how devastating and cruel the offense is. And I unflaggingly assert this punishment befits the crime. We consistently run public service announcements that encourage persons who suffer with various addictions: drug abuse, alcohol, or gambling to call a 1-800 number for help. Likewise, we can run that same public service announcement to encourage people to seek help if they find themselves attracted and/or desirous of children in this unnatural manner. An ounce of prevention is most assuredly better than a pound of cure.

I'm confident there are many doctors and/or therapists that believe pedophiles can be treated. We should seize the opportunity to reach out to potential offenders BEFORE they commit this abominable act. Children are our most precious commodity; a child is the most wonder blessing with which the Lord can bless you. It is critically incumbent upon us to better protect our children.

Chapter 4

PRISONS/CORRECTIONS

"The degree of civilization in a society can be judged by observing its prisons." (Fyodor Dostoyevsky, *Crime & Punishment*)

The three hundred million or so people in the United States of America represent approximately 4.4% of the world's population. Our prisons house a little more than two million prisoners, and that represents approximately 22% of the world's prison population. Black Americans constitute approximate 13% of the nation's population. However, more than 50% of the imprisoned population is black. All too often, a person will spend more time in prison for trafficking illegal drugs than murdering a person. According to the U.S. Bureau of Justice Statistics, there is a 76% recidivism rate for state prisoners and a 45% recidivism rate for federal prisoners. Our juvenile justice system serves more like a petri dish for the adult system than a system of guidance and correction.

In the 1700s, our prisons utilized indentured servitude, public humiliation, and ducking stools. In the 1800s, the concept of parole began as the prisons were becoming overcrowded, and additional space was needed. Eastern State Penitentiary was established just outside Philadelphia, PA with the promise of rehabilitating inmates. The founders of this prison believed that a system of solitary confinement would provide the opportunity for offenders to contemplate their misdeeds and begin a period of penance for their sins. The first prison strictly for women was opened in Indiana in 1873. In 1899, our nation came to recognize it had to address a growing juvenile delinquency problem, and juvenile court was established. Of course, the goal of the juvenile justice system was to rehabilitate the juvenile offender via vocational training and academic programs. In 1945, the prevailing ideology was offenders suffered from some sort of illness, and "medical treatment" would be the appropriate course of action to address their criminal tendencies. As penology continued to evolve by 1967, theorists introduced community-based corrections with the emphasis being placed on the deinstitutionalization of the prison system; and in 1980, patience with rehabilitation had grown thin, so warehousing inmates became the new strategy. At present, I believe it's safe to conclude a potpourri of tactics is being utilized in prisons/corrections facilities across the nation. Given the recidivism rate, we must accept the fact our strategy or strategies requires an overhaul.

On my final night in Marine Corps basic training, boot camp, after the lights were turned off, our senior drill instructor walked through the squad bay talking to us about our three months in boot camp and what to expect in the Fleet Marine Force. Gunnery Sergeant Stein entertained a few questions from us, and one question garnered a response I will never forget. One of the recruits asked Gunnery Sergeant Stein, "Sir, when will the saltpeter wear off?" Saltpeter supposedly was given to recruits while in basic training to subdue or deaden sexual urges. Gunnery Sergeant Stein responded, "Son, we haven't given you any saltpeter; we just worked your ass so hard that Suzy Rottencrotch never entered your mind." There are twenty-four hours in a day, and in Marine Corps basic training, the recruits are allowed eight hours sleep. However, the other sixteen hours belong to the drill instructors. Each day was structured in such manner as to keep the recruits involved in organized activities that met various training goals. Even group disciplinary activities were scheduled, such as having the entire platoon performing bends and thrusts in a nearby sandpit for some sort of group violation. Gunnery Sergeant Stein could not have been more correct when he stated that at day's end, we were much too tired to think of anything but sleep.

2 THESSALONIANS 3:10 (King James Version)

"For even when we were with you, this we commanded you, that if any would not work, neither should he eat."

The Thirteenth Amendment of the U.S. Constitution states in part: "Neither slavery or involuntary servitude, except as a punishment for crime whereof the party shall have been duly convicted, shall exist within the United States, or any place subject to their jurisdiction." For our purposes, the section that reads, "except as punishment for crime whereof the party shall have been duly convicted" is most salient. In Ava DuVernay's Academy Award nominated documentary, *13th*. I believe she seeks to make the case that the Thirteenth Amendment did not end slavery, it merely redefined it. She chronicles how the mass incarceration of former slaves for seemingly petty offenses was utilized to answer the demand for free labor. In my opinion, the overall inference of DuVernay's film is that the prison system became the new vehicle for enslaving America's black population, the black male in particular. The fact that approximately 50% of America's prison population is a damning fact given the reality that only 13% of the American population is black. A report generated by the U.S. Department of Justice on July 1, 2015 indicates 40% of white males are arrested by age twenty-three; seventy million American citizens have criminal records. It is not my intention to downplay the glaring disparity that exists between non-white arrestees and whites, but I believe it is noteworthy to acknowledge that approximately 23% of the American population has a criminal record. Of the two million people in American prisons, 28% have a life sentence and an additional 4% are on death row. Therefore, 68% will be returning to our communities. A sad and frustrating truth is according to the Bureau of Prisons, 76% of state inmates will reoffend; they will commit crime again and be incarcerated…AGAIN! Forty-six percent of federal prisoners find their way back to prison. By any standard, one can imagine our "corrections" system is failing miserably. Our recidivism rates are embarrassingly high. I believe there are three factors that contribute to such. (1) Prison is entirely TOO comfortable. (2) After release, former inmates are frustrated by the various roadblocks to respectability. (3) Some people are hopelessly incorrigible and will never sincerely seek to live an honest life.

(1) Prison can be entirely too comfortable. In chapter 1, I stated that during my professional career, I have encountered a number of twenty, thirty, forty and fifty-year-old boys. Specifically, I assert these males have not matured to adulthood as they were raised in an environment that enabled them to consistently avoid responsibility. They believe manhood is achieved by reaching a certain age or demonstrating physical superiority. However, these "men" have never had a lease or mortgage in their names. It is my contention that manhood is achieved only after the individual can demonstrate how responsible he is: responsibility defines a man. And then in some cases, these adult "boys" are housed in institutions that supports their immaturity. There are prisons in our country that are operated more like an Adult Day Care Center as opposed to a penal institution. The term "corrections" infers that the goal of these institutions is to teach/train the offender a more disciplined and law-abiding way of life. Those institutions which fail to consistently hold their inmates accountable are failing the inmates they house and the communities they are supposed to serve. Our court system is fraught with opportunities to dodge full responsibility for crimes committed: exclusionary rule, plea bargains, percentage sentencing, reduction in time for good behavior, etc. Most offenders never suffer the full brunt of the law for the crimes they commit. They are never made to experience the complete consequences of their misdeeds. Additionally, there are people that spend more time in federal prison for drug offenses than persons convicted of murder in a state system. In general, a person convicted of transporting a quantity of illegal drugs across state lines will spend more time in federal prison than a person sentenced to twenty years in prison for second-degree murder in a state prison.

There is a great disparity in the operations of prisons nationwide. At some prisons, the rules are fairly strict, inmate movement is limited, and security is tight. At others, the security is somewhat lax, the inmates exercise significant influence in the daily operations, and they enjoy a great deal of movement. In some prisons, the inmates can successfully protest their housing assignments. The introduction of illegal drugs into any prison in America is a felony, and at some prisons, visitors who attempt to do such are arrested and prosecuted accordingly. At other prisons, the culprit is briefly detained, placed on the banned list and then released. In some prisons, most of the prisoners are busy the majority of the day with various tasks or work assignments. And in others, the prisoners have little if any activities scheduled, and the inmates spend the bulk of the day watching TV and playing board games or depending upon the weather in the "yard" on rec call. The prisoners have responsibility for cleaning their own areas, although some must be chided into participating. Hair and grooming are major concerns for male and female prisoners; they are afforded the opportunity to barber themselves (males) and set up semi hair salons (females). In some prisons, many inmates complain about the quality and/or quality of the food served. For those who have the means, inmates are afforded the opportunity to order snacks and drinks (commissary ordering). Additionally, there are vending machines at the disposal of inmates with means. In many institutions, the inmates can purchase meals from outside vendors. These meals are comparable to the selections found in fairly high-end carry out restaurants.

At many penitentiaries/prisons in this country, the inmates have access to exercise equipment (weights) that favorably compare to equipment utilized by Olympic athletes. Oddly enough, many public high schools and colleges do not have the revenue to provide the same quality equipment for student athletes enrolled in their institutions. In some prisons, the inmates have access to flat-screen televisions and DVD players. They spend a significant portion of their day watching television. In some institutions, the inmates have their own private televisions. If not watching television, they are playing cards, board games, talking on the telephone or just lying in bed. In many of our prisons contraband, illegal drugs and cigarettes flow freely. Cellular telephones are frequently found in our prisons. Sadly, a significant portion of the free-flowing contraband is introduced to the prison by employees. All things considered, prison life can be quite comfortable.

(2) Approximately 68% of the people incarcerated in our prisons/penitentiaries are going to be released. They will be coming back to our cities, back to our neighborhoods, and they will require a means by which to live. Each will be encumbered with a label: ex-con, ex-offender, former inmate. Options for former offenders are limited. Many employers automatically reject applications from former offenders, attaining financial aid for higher education and/or vocational education is exceptionally challenging, and securing start-up capital from most financial institutions is virtually impossible.

Inmates are admonished that upon release, they should avoid certain people, places and things that will lead them back to incarceration. The reality, however, is the vast majority of inmates released from prison come back to the place they lived before being arrested. And with limited options, the "instant gratification" culture into which this nation has devolved and the fact many have lived a life which has enabled them to eschew the responsibility of adulthood crime remains a way of life.

(3) "Free will." I believe God has instilled free will into each person mentally capable of choice. Most people will follow the path lay before them by their caregivers—the person(s) who raised them. However, there are certain individuals who will stray in spite of the most sincere and concerted efforts of their parents/caregivers. These incorrigible individuals consistently ignore/reject efforts by anyone to integrate them into lawful society. During his concert film, *Richard Pryor: Live on the Sunset Strip*, the comedian talked about the six weeks he spent at Arizona State Penitentiary filming the 1980 film *Stir Crazy*. "My heart ached as I saw all those brothers, warriors that should be out with the masses. I talked to the brothers, and I talked to the brothers, I talked to the brothers. Thank God we got penitentiaries. I asked one bruh, why did you kill everybody in the house? Bruh said they were home." The tragic reality is that God-given free will shall always produce a certain percentage of individuals that prefer the "outlaw lifestyle." In spite of efforts made by parents, caregivers, the juvenile justice system, counselors/therapists, etc., they will NEVER conform to the ways of polite society. Thank God we have penitentiaries.

It is my contention that a more effective prison system would be a more uniform prison system. We should never hear inmates comparing the accommodations of the prisons in one state to another. It should never be the case that an inmate believes he/she will have a better quality of life in the prisons of state A as opposed to the prisons of state B. I cannot and will not advocate the mistreatment of any of the prisoners, but prison should not be a pleasant or comfortable experience. The basic needs of every prisoner must and should be met; creature comforts are NOT needs. The duo purpose of our penal system is punishment for misdeeds and to provide the opportunity for self-reform. Each individual should be secure in the knowledge that prison is a lousy place to live, and he/she should aspire to never again return. There is no better way to do a wrong thing, so working to remain in compliance with the law should be paramount in the mind of every inmate. Furthermore, as much as possible, the inmates should be made to know that for many of them, the people that genuinely love them suffer in their absence. The children of inmates suffer in particular. One of the most powerful letters I've ever read was a letter sent by a six-year-old girl to her father. The letter read: "Dear Daddy, please stop selling drugs. I need you to be home to help raise me."

As I harken back to Marine Corps basic training, I remember being told that we would be "broken down and reshaped." We would be stripped of our civilian identities and remade into Marines. Stripping the inmate of his/her criminal identity should be a priority in our prison system. Therefore, in order to begin the transformation and for sanitary reasons, each inmate male and female should be shaved bald and remain so until release. Many inmates spend inordinate periods of time grooming and primping as though they are preparing for a date. Inmates that possess certain cosmetology skills curry favor with others in exchange for a particular hairstyle. Some of those same inmates operate businesses within the prison walls. They braid and/or cut hair in exchange for commissary items. Mistakes made during the grooming process lead to acts of violence. And psychologically, the inmate's hairdo can serve as a means to retain their criminal identity. It is the criminal identity that our penal system should work to eradicate.

It is a commonly accepted fact that eight hours sleep is the optimal standard for adults. Each inmate should be given the opportunity to have eight hours sleep, and unless there is a viable medical reason no more than eight-hour sleep. The other sixteen hours should be scripted with endless activity. Every hour of the inmate's incarcerated life should be scheduled/scripted. There should be absolutely zero idle time, no opportunity for extracurricular activities. At day's end, the inmate's single-minded goal should be to get into bed and get to sleep. As Senior Drill Instructor Gunnery Sergeant Stein stated, we worked so hard that at the end of the day, sleep was the only thing on your mind. I must acknowledge there will be some pushback from inmates that are too lazy to work or too defiant to follow the rules. However, capitulating to their defiance is NOT the answer. Standards of compliance must be made known, and the consequences of failing to comply with such must be enacted without exception.

Uniformity is a basic tenant in group discipline, and group discipline is essential in a prison environment. Inmates are issued uniforms to promote discipline and make them easily identifiable in the prison environment. Prison uniforms vary from institution to institution. In the institutions where pants or jeans are issued, inmates seek to retain their "street" identity by intentionally wearing oversized pants or jeans that fall below the waistline. Sagging has become the preferred style of wearing pants, and the inmates fight desperately to cling to that which identifies them with their criminal life. I believe the universal prison uniform should be jumpsuits. They should be color coded in accordance with the inmate's security level. Placing each inmate in a jumpsuit ensures the sagging problem will be eliminated. Additionally, it eliminates any opportunity for inmates of either sex to wear their uniforms too tightly and/or suggestively. Establishing and maintaining an asexual environment is critically important for our penal system.

There should be no "pecking order" within the confines of any prison: no haves and have-nots. Each inmate should have access to the exact same resources. No inmate should be in position to acquire something that is not available to each inmate. Hence, the practice of commissary purchases should be eliminated. Commissary items serve as currency within the walls; commissary items often become the cause of violence as some inmate steal or forcibly take commissary items from others. Not every inmate has family or friends that will "put money on their books," and that reality creates a harmful divide among the prisoners. Equally divisive is the availability of vending machines for the inmates. In order for this to be completely fair, we must ensure the quality and quantity of food is improved. The inmates should be fed as though they are adults. "Happy Meal" quantities are completely unacceptable. Equally important the meals must be prepared in a completely sanitary environment; there is absolutely zero excuse for the presence of roaches and/or rodents in food preparation or storage areas. Each facility has the undeniable responsibility for providing food for its inmates. Upgrading the menu and quantity is essential in an environment where commissary items and vending machines do not exist. Additionally, this provides the institution with a vehicle for disciplining noncompliant inmates. Inmates that violate institution rules can be segregated and fed separately from the main, compliant population. The violators should be fed nutritious, but less appealing meals. They of course should be afforded eight hours sleep daily but should not be left with the choice of lying in bed vegetating. Regimented structure and discipline is critically important to any successful penal institution.

Most retail theft is committed by employees; most of the contraband introduced into a penal institution is done so by employees. In some facilities, security is tight, and breaching such is challenging. In others, the security is laughable at best, and the contraband is free flowing. In many penal institutions, certain inmates are awarded the privilege of leaving the compound for various work details. Some are compensated with a bonus deduction from their sentence, still others are financially compensated. Some inmates are escorted to and from the facility with security personnel; others are escorted by civilian personnel. Yes, I wrote civilians. There are some institutions that provide armed escorts and others the escorts are unarmed. Communication devices for the escorts vary from institution to institution. There are institutions that prohibit the possession of any cellular telephone device by the escorts. Their escorts, civilian and security carry only a radio which is limited to communication with the prison. These escorts cannot notify local law enforcement in any manner; they are completely dependent upon the prison's dispatch system. In some instances, inmates are escorted to areas of town where they can have direct contact with the town's populace. In other words, they are assigned work assignments in places where friends and/or family members can meet up with them and bring just about anything to them. And oh yes, the unarmed escort with a communication device that is limited to the prison is charged with the responsibility of ensuring the inmate does not interact with the friends/family members that come to the site and ensuring the inmate does not receive any items from said friends/family. The security issues are numerous and BGO (blinding glimpse of the obvious). It is my contention that any penal institution which sends inmates off the compound with unarmed escorts equipped with limited communication devices is needlessly placing the escort, inmates, and the general public in peril. Regardless of the inmate's security level or how thoroughly one may believe the inmate has been vetted, circumstances can arise that will cloud the judgment of most any person. Furthermore, there will always be a percentage of the prison population which will display the necessary front to attain privilege and use such for nefarious ends: collection and distribution of contraband most notably.

It is my contention that a singular, unarmed individual possessing a limited communication device should NEVER be charged with the supervision of ANY number of inmates outside the confines of a penal institution. Furthermore, civilians should NEVER have the responsibility of supervising inmates outside the walls of a prison. Arrestees that require medical attention are not left in the custody of civilians: a sworn law enforcement officer assumes that responsibility. Hospital security is not charged with that responsibility. Hence, the idea of a civilian supervising a person(s) who has been CONVICTED, not merely arrested, but CONVICTED is befuddling. Any detail of prisoners outside the walls of a prison should be supervised by a minimum of two armed officers possessing communication devices with which they can make direct contact with local law enforcement. The security level of the prisoners, their disciplinary history or the offense for which they were convicted should dictate how they are supervised outside the confines of the institution. There's not one person in prison for singing too loudly in the choir and underestimating that of which they are capable is foolhardy.

Prison life offers a myriad of opportunities for self-improvement; at least for those motivated to sincerely apply themselves. Inmates are given the opportunity to complete high school equivalency standards (in some states, completion of such is mandatory), earn vocational educational certificates, complete therapeutic groups and learn basic life skills (balancing a checkbook, budgeting, parenting, etc.). Some inmates are actually placed in employment opportunities upon release, and some take full advantage of such. Still others squander the opportunity and return to a life of crime. One inescapable truth is that convicted felons face a daunting task as they attempt to integrate into society. The poor choice(s) they make which leads to their incarceration severely limits options after release. Most find themselves in a small box with scant few opportunities; however, they have the same or similar aspirations as the rest of society. They most assuredly have the same basic needs: food, clothing, shelter, and health care. Many have family obligations, and let's remember the children of the convicted felons did not commit any crimes and should not be held responsible for the irresponsible behavior of the adult(s) who parented them.

I will begin by stating that there is no easy fix for the problem of integrating convicted felons back into society. It is seemingly unfair that society as a whole should bear the responsibility of the ex-offender's children. And there really is no perfect vehicle to provide for the children and force the parent(s) into their rightful role as provider and nurturer. But when we fail to assist the children that can be saved, when we fail to make available the possibility for the ex-offender to earn his/her way back into law-abiding society, we contribute mightily to the never-ending cycle of recidivism and increased index crime. Index crime is a drain on our society and has a negative impact upon the quality of life for each of us. Current technology has made it impossible to escape the ravages of crime by moving to the suburbs or a small "Mayberry-like" town. This is a problem we must face head-on and conquer. One step in that direction is to provide the opportunity for select convicted felons to earn the privilege of having their criminal convictions expunged and the full restoration of their civil liberties. I propose that persons convicted of nonviolent crimes should have the opportunity to have their criminal convictions expunged after five years of crime-free living. They must be able to demonstrate they are employed or operating a viable business. If they are employed part-time and in school or training for an eventual career, that too shall suffice. Additionally, they must be able to show they are meeting each of the responsibilities owed to any children to whom they are a parent. The fee for expungement must not be overwhelming, it should not exceed $250.00; however, the burden of proof must fall completely upon the applicant. The cost of fingerprint analysis should be met by the applicant, and he/she should be responsible for providing check stubs and tax returns to verify their legitimate source(s) of income. It is a simple matter for the applicant to provide a transcript which demonstrates he/she is making progress toward the completion of a scholastic or vocational degree. I do not suggest that this process be made easy, it has to be earned. We must make the applicant commit and work diligently to meet the criteria. However, he/she must see the light at the end of the tunnel, thereby recognizing that attainment of such is possible. The applicant and his/her family will benefit, and overall, our society benefits as we will be taking in additional productive citizens. We will be providing an opportunity to break the cycle of criminality which serves as an unhealthy burden upon us all.

During an inmate's period of incarceration, he/she has the opportunity to participate in various therapeutic groups which are designed to assist a motivated inmate with making the necessary internal changes to remain free of incarceration once released. Alcoholics Anonymous (AA) is a perfect example of such. However, unlike many of the other therapeutic groups, AA offers continued therapy once the inmate has been released. One can find an AA group all over this nation. I believe the factor that gives AA more credibility than some other groups is that each of the participants has a drinking problem. Every person in attendance has personal experiences with the horrors of alcoholism. Anger management is one of the more prominent therapeutic groups offered in the prison system, and the basic concept of assisting people reach the point where they control their emotions as opposed to being controlled by emotion is an invaluable tool. However, unlike AA, a plentiful network of these therapeutic groups outside the walls of the prison system does not exist. Dr. Gregory Little and Dr. Kenneth Robinson developed Moral Reconation Therapy (MRT), a systematic treatment strategy that seeks to decrease recidivism among juvenile and adult criminal offenders by increasing moral reasoning. Once the client has been released, there are scarce few opportunities to pursue follow-up for the initial treatment. The success AA has enjoyed is due to the fact continued therapy is a constant; it is always available. Additionally, the facilitators have instant credibility as they too are recovering alcoholics. I submit therapeutic groups (MRT, anger management, et al) facilitated by former inmates can enjoy success similar to AA. There are individuals among us that would eagerly seize upon the opportunity to provide this service if/when possible.

"It is easier to build strong children than to repair broken men" (Frederick Douglass).

There exists a strong relationship between high school graduation rates, scholastic achievement and index crime. According to the Bureau of Justice Statistics, over 70% of the American inmate population cannot read above a fourth grade level. Given that reality, there is no real opportunity for these people to find gainful employment, successfully operate a legitimate business, succeed in our society. The majority of the blame for this atrocity falls squarely upon the shoulders of the parents. The parents fail to train the child properly so that he/she knows how to conduct themselves in school. The parents fail to make scholastic achievement a priority: school is just a babysitter. Parents fail to hold their children responsible for little; in fact, they ENABLE them to avoid the maturation process. The "No Child Left Behind" campaign contributed mightily to a substandard system which fails to hold students and their parents accountable for academic achievement. As test scores declined and the failure rate increased, then President George W. Bush came to the conclusion that "dumbing down" the educational system was the answer. This is illustrated in a report generated in 2015 by the Pew Research Center. Pew reports that in comparison to students from other nations, our children rank 24th in science, 39th in Math, and 24th in reading. Training the children for "the test" and then dropping the expectations serves the student in no way at all. The Organization for Economic Cooperation and Development (OECD) developed the Program for the International Assessment of Adult Competencies (PIAAC), an academic test for this generation's young adults (the millennials). Our young adults ranked dead last in academic achievement in comparison to their counterparts in the other industrialized nations.

Mathematics is probably the purest form of logic: one plus one is two in any language. It is my belief that long division serves as the first exercise in problem-solving during a child's academic career. However, many school systems in our country have ceased teaching this basic skill. The April 2000 issue of *American School Board Journal* featured an article written by David Klein entitled "Math Problems: Why the Department of Education's Recommended Math Problems Don't Add Up." Following is part of that text:

Disagreements over math curricula are often portrayed as "basic skills versus conceptual understanding." Scientists and mathematicians, including many who signed the open letter to Secretary Riley (Richard Riley, Secretary of Education under Pres. George W. Bush) are described as advocates of basic skills, while professional educators are counted as proponents of conceptual understanding. Ironically, such a portrayal ignores the deep conceptual understanding of mathematics held by mathematicians. But more important, the notion that conceptual understanding in mathematics can be separated from precision fluency in the execution of basic skills is just plain wrong.

In other domains of human activity, such as athletics or music, the dependence of high levels of performance on requisite skills goes unchallenged. A novice cannot hope to achieve mastery in martial arts without first learning basic katas or exercises in movement.

Essentially, the author is stating it is imperative that a person masters the basic fundamentals of an endeavor before he/she can become proficient in that endeavor. Michael Jordan, Earvin "Magic" Johnson, and Larry Bird became Hall of Fame basketball players because they had mastered the basic fundamentals of the game. Sheer athletic ability is insufficient to play the game at the level in which they played. It is my contention that failing to teach our children long division adversely affects the development of problem-solving skills, and problem-solving skills have a direct impact upon the decisions that people make. People do not go to jail because of mistakes; mistakes are accidents. Poor decisions lead to criminal acts: we must foster critical thinking skills. Doing such will equip our children with skills necessary to make rational choices.

One of the most disconcerting realities in our country is the level of violence that exists in our schools. I believe the playground "push and shove" or the occasional punch 'em out has existed in schools as long as there have been children attending schools. However, the introduction of firearms to this equation completely changed the landscape. The armed child does not realize the gun provides permanent solutions to temporary problems. In the 7th Police District in Chicago, we had to provide substantial police presence at dismissal for each of the high schools in the district to avert daily violence. In spite of the fact metal detectors were present in each of the high schools, the threat of shootings remained a very real possibility. At times, a dispute would develop between some students, and one of the disputants would leave school during the middle of the school day. That same student would come back to the area of the school at dismissal with a firearm to settle the dispute. I came to the conclusion that something more had to be done. During my tenure on the Local School Council, I sat in on several parent-teacher conferences. Sadly, tragically, I witnessed parents ask the teacher, "What ya'll teaching him here? He acts the same way at home," in response when the teacher informed the parent of how badly the child behaved in school. Given that reality, I came to the conclusion that it would be an exercise in futility if we attempted to launch a campaign against the violence in the schools that was exclusively dependent upon parental involvement.

As I reflected upon my twelve years in the Chicago Catholic School System, I thought of the twelve years of mandatory religion or theology classes I took. It was at that point I developed the idea that curricula should be developed for a mandatory twelve years of instruction in conflict resolution. I believe it is imperative that we train our children to resolve conflict absent violence in any manner—physical, verbal, or otherwise. And perhaps the key to such is developing the skill of listening. Sure, we hear what the other person is saying, but how well do we listen to what is being said? Is it more often true than not that we listen to what the other person is saying just long enough to interject what we believe is most relevant, to put forth our view as in our opinion only our view has merit? What is most assuredly true is when we approach a dispute in that manner the message delivered is the other person's view is unimportant and thusly so is the other person. The person receiving this message feels marginalized, becomes defensive and is likely to hold fast to his/her viewpoint regardless of any fact(s) presented. I drafted a letter to the superintendent of Chicago Schools at that time, Arne Duncan, with hope this idea would be considered. I waited a month and sent follow-up correspondence and received ZERO acknowledgment of such. Arne Duncan later became Secretary of Education under President Barack Obama. I cannot state that Mr. Duncan ever received the correspondence I sent to his attention; I know that it was sent to the correct address. Furthermore, I know there was never an attempt to develop my suggestion. I am convinced that if we were to incorporate conflict resolution into the curricula for students in grades one thru twelve, there will be a significant opportunity to experience a dramatic effect upon our crime rate. Training children to respect one another, listen to one another thereby solving disputes in a nonconfrontational and civil manner will have a dramatic effect upon violent crime. Classes in conflict resolution will assist in the development of critical thinking and problem-solving. Training young people to put emotion aside in the midst of a dispute and solving that dispute rationally is an invaluable life skill. Hearing is a physical ability, listening is a skill. When we listen to the other person we convey the message their concerns have value, they have merit, even if we disagree with such. I submit may disagreements will not devolve into negative confrontations if the opposing parties make one another feel their view(s), thus the individual has value.

The late comedian George Carlin quipped that the "true owners" of this country, the heads of the ultrapowerful corporations are starkly against the development of critical thinking. He joked about this "big club, and you ain't in it" during one of his performances. He went on to discuss how the "true owners" want the populous to be just educated enough to push the correct buttons and complete the paperwork efficiently, but critical thinking is a skill they need not have. If a majority of "we the people" have critical thinking skills, we'll recognize just how badly we are being treated by the "true owners" of this country. And recognition of such will cut dramatically into the profit margin for the country's "true owners."

"The average reading level for five of the top seven books assigned as summer reading by 341 colleges using Renaissance Learning's readability formula was rated 7.56" (Dr. Sandra Stotsky). Dr. Stotsky developed one of our nation's strongest sets of academic standards for K-12 students in her capacity as Senior Associate Commissioner for the Massachusetts Department of Education. According to Dr. Stotsky, at least 341 colleges have "dumbed down" admissions standards for incoming freshmen to the point where they aren't expected to read even at a high school level. I foresee a time when the degrees earned at some colleges will not be worth the paper upon which they are printed. It is a commonly accepted fact that lack of basic education is a major contributing factor to index crime. As our nation continues to relax educational standards, demand less of its students and continue to be satisfied with training students to pass standardized tests as opposed to TEACHING them a new segment of the population will become crop for the "prison industry." I believe the combination of retail-driven economy, young adults with an "instant gratification" work ethic and a job market which demands aptitude and ability for which these young adults are bereft will augment the criminal class. I foresee a time when inadequately educated young people will turn to crime to attain the additional income necessary to buy the latest hi-tech gizmos, latest clothing fashions and hottest new vehicles. This of course is not new to our country as the prisons are full of such people at present. The difference I envision is that young people that complete a substandard educational experience will turn to crime. They will be frustrated by the reality they've completed what society has promoted as the pathway to gainful employment: the type of which is replete with above average salary compensation and benefits only to learn they are ill prepared for the current job market. I submit that failing to adequately train and educate our youth is analogous to sentencing them to prison.

"Beware the Industrial Military Complex," warned President Dwight David Eisenhower in 1961. He was concerned that the introduction of civilian contractors to the American defense system would corrupt our national defense. He envisioned that the focus of our Defense Department would become creating revenue for civilian contractors as opposed to protecting our nation. I am going to extrapolate that sentiment into a discussion regarding private prisons. It is my contention that when a state seeks to abdicate its responsibility for the operation of any part of its prison/corrections system, it does a grave injustice to its citizens. The primary objective of any privately run business is to make money. Creating capitol is NOT the function of a prison or corrections facility. Businesses are built around produce, commodities; human beings are not commodities. The very essence of corrections is to deter offenders from criminality; hence, defeating recidivism and reducing the prison population. In stark contrast, the optimal reality for the business of private prisons is for the recidivism rate to increase, thus providing more "crop" for the private prison industry. The state of Arizona is defending itself against a lawsuit brought against it for failing to provide a sufficient number of inmates. There is no possible scenario in which an increase of inmates benefits a state. The ultimate goal of our CORRECTIONS system is to guide the inmate into a law-abiding lifestyle: our society seeks to change the arc upon which the offender is traveling not further it. The idea of CORRECTIONS is to assist offenders in the transformation to responsible law-abiding citizenship. The prison system does not benefit from an increased population and/or an obscene recidivism rate. However, for the private prison industry to thrive, an increased prison population is critically necessary.

It appears as though two factors were the catalyst for the emergence of the private prison industry. (1) The skyrocketing costs of operating a prison. In this nation, the average cost of incarcerating one person in a state facility for a year is $31,286. (2) The ever-burgeoning recidivism rate; according to the U.S. Bureau of Justice Statistics, the five-year recidivism rate for state inmates is 76.6%. This represents a lousy return on our tax dollar investment. The federal recidivism rate of 44.7% is appreciably better than the state level; perhaps because there is more uniformity in the manner in which those prisons are operated. It would be easy to criticize the state corrections personnel, but I strongly believe such criticism would be unfair and inaccurate. The "few" miscreants in any group always tarnish the honorable majority. We cannot turn a blind eye to the misconduct of the few, but we have to acknowledge that most of the employees do not violate laws and serve honorably. We can improve the performance of our state-run penal systems by enacting the following measures:

1. Revise the recruitment and training process. There should be an outside, out-of-state agency assigned the responsibility of recruiting and training corrections employees. The training should be just as stressful as the "Marine Corps" like training I've suggested for police officers. True character will surface in stressful situations.

2. An outside, out-of-state agency should be charged with the responsibility of selecting staff members for promotion. This should include administrators. There should NEVER be a promotion granted based upon the "people" an applicant knows as opposed to that applicant's aptitude and ability. Political favoritism, patronage and/or crony-

ism should have ZERO effect upon the selection of any administrator.

3. The Internal Affairs Department of every state prison should report directly to the state prosecutor. The director/ warden of any prison should not have authority over this department. No employee is above reproach, and sadly, some administrators have violated the laws and policies of a particular state. Internal Affairs should be free to monitor each employee regardless of his/her rank.

4. There must be a strict antifraternization policy; any institution that allows persons of higher rank to become romantically involved with subordinates invites the worst kind of trouble. It is commonplace in this world for persons of superior rank to use said rank to intimidate employees and attempt to force them into unwanted "personal" relationships. There has been some advancement regarding this practice, but we cannot ignore the fact that some still attempt to utilize this practice. We must also not ignore the fact that some subordinates will attempt to seduce a person of superior rank to gain favor for work assignments, days off, promotions, etc.

5. There should be drug-sniffing dogs at each entrance and exit of the facility. Every employee, contractor, volunteer or visitor should have to pass the drug-sniffing dogs. Random searches by Internal Affairs should be the policy at each penal institution, and from this practice, NO ONE is exempt.

6. There must be strict enforcement of laws that prohibit the exposure of a person's genitals to another for the purpose of self-gratification. Such behavior is a criminal offense in each of the fifty states, and it should be enforced as such WITHOUT fail. The offender must be rearrested and criminally charged in each instance. There is a clear distinction between an inmate having a private moment in his/her quarters and one that intentionally targets passersby for a peep show. Tragically, some institutions treat

this matter as just a normal workplace occurrence. These institutions fail to recognize they are complicit in the inmate's bad behavior; and the targeted group of employees, usually women, could find success in a class action lawsuit in federal court. The failure to adequately address this matter constitutes creating a hostile work environment for those employees.

7. In many states, the primary prison is located in a small town, several hours away from the largest metropolis of the state. Most of the inmates naturally originate from the state's largest cities. In many cases, these states have had to build additional prisons in different parts of the state to accommodate the ever-growing prison population. And in some of these states, a prison has been opened in a midsized metropolis; and the convicted felons from said midsized metropolis are sentenced to that "hometown" prison. The most important aspect of any penal institution is security. Absent stringent security a penal institution is something akin to sleepaway camp. An unfortunate reality of "hometown" prisons with midsized cities is many of the inmates and staff know one another. Some attended school together, are neighbors or family members, perhaps even former or current lovers. Some inmates know deeply personal facts about certain staff members. This reality provides far too many opportunities for breaches of security. The remedy for this is to have inmates from Town A imprisoned in the facility in Town B and vice versa. This could represent a hardship on the family and friends of the inmates, but security has to take precedence over convenience for inmates and their visitors. Nothing is more important than ensuring the security of the penal institution.

8. Tragically, many of our nation's penal institutions are dangerously understaffed. There is a myriad of reasons for this, the most obvious being a lack of funding. Given the responsibility of corrections professionals, the salaries are

not commensurate with the task. Staff shortages contribute to ineffective communication at times as the institutions cannot utilize staggered shifts: this practice would ensure the opportunity for roll call before each shift and an effective sharing of information from the previous shift. In some states, corrections professionals are considered "protected" employees. Along with police officers, teachers, firefighters, hospital personnel, and transit employees, these employees are deemed essential to the fabric of the society they serve. Hence, any physical assault upon those employees during the commission of their duties is AUTOMATICALLY considered a felony. Attacks upon "protected" employees should be prosecuted as felonies WITHOUT EXCEPTION nationwide. This should be the standard in each of the fifty states, and there should be absolutely ZERO wiggle room for the prosecution or judge. We must assure the men and women that work in these essential public service jobs that their service and sacrifice is most assuredly treasured. Furthermore, the incorrigibles who choose to attack these treasured employees should be made to understand there is a stringent penalty for their mindless acts.

9. There must be consistency in supervision and leadership. Every institution must be ACTUALLY policy driven and MUST adhere to such regardless of which supervisor is on duty. Consistency is an essential component in any successful organization. Personalities should NEVER be a factor in the operations of a penal organization. Every class of employee must be valued and treated accordingly. If management demonstrates even the slightest bias in favor of on group of employees, an atmosphere of distrust will be created and nurtured by such. It is critically important that the employees work with a sense of esprit de corps, commitment to one another. The failure of management to promote such demonstrates a crisis for leadership in that facility. Competent management will seek to identify

,duals within their organization that possess quali-
,ons, aptitude and ability to bolster the efficiency of
,r prison and promote them into leadership and/or spe-
lized positions. Employees with special skill sets and/or
,vanced education should be viewed as assets as opposed
to potential threats to the established management (suits).

Operating a penal institution should not be a profit-driven exercise. I recognize that as long as there will always be those persons that violate the laws of the land, and we as a society must be prepared to deal with the offenders. However, they ARE human and not commodities; some of them can be salvaged. And if we entrust this responsibility to those who profit only when there is an abundance of inmates, we abdicate our responsibility to society as a whole.

MENTALLY ILL IN PRISON

"Whatsoever you do to the least of MY brothers: that you do unto ME."

According to the Bureau of Justice Statistics, 56% of state inmates have "some" degree of mental illness, 45% of federal inmates are afflicted with such, and 64% of the inmates in county jails have some degree of mental disease. Thirteen percent of mentally ill inmates were homeless at the time they were arrested. Before we go further, it is important to note that these figures are based upon voluntary interviews of inmates housed in prisons and jails nationwide. And it is equally noteworthy that this data does not represent inmates who opted not to participate in the interview process or were incapable of participating in the interview process. The Bureau of Justice Statistics reports approximately 11% of the U.S. population ages eighteen or over suffers from some sort of mental health problem. This does NOT mean these people are incapable of living self-sufficient, crime-free lives. There are varied degrees of mental disorder, and many persons suffering from such can function in a responsible and productive manner with proper mental health care.

In 1979, President Jimmy Carter signed into law legislation that would provide funding for long-term mental health facilities. He and Congress determined that it was necessary to provide housing and long-term care for those mentally incapable of caring for themselves. In 1980, President Ronald Reagan killed that funding and dumped those mentally ill people onto the street. Not one of the presidents who succeeded Reagan addressed this matter. According to The Treatment Advocacy Center, an estimated 33% of this nation's homeless population is mentally ill. They suffer from assorted afflictions to include schizophrenia, schizoaffective disorder, bipolar disorder, and major depression. As a result, the prison system has become the de facto long-term mental health facility. The mentally ill homeless person waffles back and forth between victim/offender until he/she dies or is arrested. Penal institutions do not function as mental health treatment facilities, and it is not feasible that they should be expected to operate as such. The objective of mental health units in a correctional facility is to ensure that inmates with mental health issues are able to serve their sentences in a safe manner. The mental health professionals assess the condition of a client and provide appropriate medication where necessary and/or ensure the inmate is housed in the most appropriate environment to address his/her illness. Therapeutic treatment is not the objective; ensuring the inmate completes his/her sentence with as few incidents as possible is the goal. One tragic truth is that mentally ill persons who were homeless at the time of their arrest shall be homeless when their sentences are complete. Homeless shelters are ill equipped to meet the needs/challenges of the mentally ill. Therefore, the cycle continues: the homeless mentally ill person shall continue on this "hamster wheel" cycle until death. In some prisons, the homeless, mentally ill person is discharged back into the public without any "real" clothing or a place to live. In these institutions, the clothing of the incoming inmate is mailed to that person's home address. There is no consideration for the homeless person, and he/she is released after their sentence has expired absent clothing, penniless, and of course, HOMELESS. The result of such is quite predictable. This is part of the hard, cold reality for the mentally ill in our Judeo-Christian nation.

It is not my intention to criticize the mental health units or mental health professionals in our nation's prison system. Some of our penal institutions have better facilities for inmates with mental difficulties than others. In these institutions, the mentally ill have programs in place for their specific needs. But even if each prison in our nation was able to develop the requisite accommodations for our nation's mentally ill, they should not have to go to prison for the care their illness requires. The prison system should not be the long-term mental health facility for our nation. We must reestablish long-term care facilities for the mentally ill; it is our rightful duty as a nation. The criteria for involuntary commitment to a mental institution must be amended; if a person suffers from a mental disease that permanently inhibits his/her ability to care for themselves, they should be subject to involuntary commitment to a mental health facility. If a person's mental disease leaves he/she absent the wherewithal to live and function in a responsible and self-sufficient manner, that person should not be abandoned by our society.

Suicide Precaution

Every correctional facility, prison and/or jail is responsible for the health, safety and well-being of its inmates. Each penal institution has a policy for addressing instances of self-harm or the threat of such. Most often the inmate in question is secluded from the general population and staff members conduct frequent wellness checks to ensure the inmate has not committed an act of self-harm. These inmates remain in secluded custody until a mental health professional concludes the inmate is no longer a threat to themselves or others. A major detriment in that assessment is what the inmate verbally communicates to the mental health professional. Given this reality manipulative inmates utilize this policy to evade disciplinary actions, force a change of housing assignment or to evade conflict with other inmates. Incorrigible inmates who are close to the completion of their sentences will assault a staff member, destroy property or commit other violations of institutional rules, then exclaim, "I'm feeling suicidal" and avoid any consequence for their misdeeds. In some cases the administrators are all too willing to acquiesce with this strategy just to get the problem inmate out of the institution. What is glaringly missing in this strategy is any sincere effort at correcting the troublemaker. Instead the miscreant is passed along, never held accountable for his/her misdeeds and deposited back into the community. These manipulators misuse valuable resources that should be directed to inmates that are genuinely troubled and sincerely pose a threat to themselves. There should be no policy that rewards the inmate for bad behavior and provides an avenue of escape for any violation of policy. The overall purpose of establishing prisons, jails and/or correctional facilities is to decisively handle the law breakers. These facilities should never pass along or dodge responsibility for punishing their rule breakers.

Chapter 5

WINNING THE WAR ON DRUGS

Our nation has been seeking a solution for the illegal use and trafficking of illicit drugs since the 1870s. In the 1870s, antiopium laws were enacted to address the opium/heroin epidemic with which this nation struggled. In the early 1900s, cocaine became our nation's target; and in 1910, the new villainous drug was marijuana. However, it wasn't until 1971 when President Richard M. Nixon made it official that the "war on drugs" began. President Nixon's declaration of war evolved from the development of synthetic drugs, mainly LSD. And in more recent years, the nation has experienced the scourge of methamphetamine, ecstasy, hydro cannabis, et al. Illegal drugs have evolved and developed with our technological advances. In spite of our efforts, the millions of man-hours, billions of dollars and overall public crusade we are no closer to winning this war on drugs than we were in 1870. An example of the futility in our efforts is that Americans are four times more likely to use cocaine in our lifetime (16% of the population) than any other nation in the world: this according to the World Health Organization.

"Those who do not know history are doomed to repeat it" is not a cliché. We can point to events in world history that illustrate this fact in glaring fashion. Adolph Hitler's attempt to conquer Russia provides a glaring example of such. Had he spent a wee bit more time learning European history as opposed to spewing his hateful rhetoric he would have learned the futility of attacking Russia in the dead of winter. The Russians did not defeat Napoleon, the Russian winter did. When Hitler failed to adequately supply his troops during the winter of their Russian crusade, they met the same fate. (Thank goodness.) Hitler was either ignorant of history or arrogantly decided to defy history. His folly in Russia was a major contributing factor to his ultimate defeat.

In January 1920, the Eighteenth Amendment to the Constitution, the Volstead Act was signed into law. This amendment was enacted to address what the nation believed to be the scourge of our nation—alcoholic beverages. Alcoholic beverages led to a disproportionate number of deaths and assaulted the moral fiber of our nation. Alcoholic beverages were evil and had to be eliminated. This vile substance attacked our weaknesses and adversely impacted upon our nation's productivity. Beer, wine and whiskey created alcoholics and destroyed families. The feeling was that these "devil's brews" could be legislated out of existence, removed from our country, and the quality of life would be enhanced. The result of legislation was the complete antisepsis of its intent. Prohibition led to the most violent period in this country since Manifest Destiny and the establishment of the "Wild, Wild West." It became the lifeblood of organized crime; it invigorated the nation's criminal element. The crime bosses had an understanding of human frailty and knew the Criminal Justice System could not abate the demand for alcoholic beverages. Mob kingpins began stockpiling alcoholic beverages when the concept was initially introduced in anticipation of the eventual success of this legislation. They knew such legislation would provide a bonanza of opportunity for them, and that preparation for such was frugal. Highly organized points of manufacture and distribution were established, and "The Mob" flourished during this period. However, the violence that accompanies this type of illicit activity rose exponentially. Alcoholic consumption did NOT decrease, alcoholism was not solved, and our nation's productivity did not increase. The prison population increased, crime rate raised, and our quality of life was adversely affected. The only entity that benefited from the Volstead Act was the criminal faction of our society. In 1930, Congress acknowledged the folly in this endeavor and drafted the Twenty-First Amendment to the Constitution which repealed the Volstead Act. Organized crime experienced a brief hiccup as it had begun preparation for the eventual reversal of the Eighteenth Amendment: "The Mob" went "all in" with the illegal drug trade.

The United States has approximately 4.4% of the world's population, but by far is the largest market for illegal drugs on the planet. The illegal drug trade is a multitrillion-dollar-a-year industry, and Americans are its most anxious customers. A report by RAND, Drug Policy Research Center for the Office on National Drug Control Policy indicates that Americans spent approximately one trillion dollars on illegal drugs between 2000 and 2010. Our government spends anywhere between forty and fifty billion dollars a year on drug enforcement, but the expenditure on illegal drugs remains a constant.

Marijuana has been legalized in some form in twenty-nine states plus the District of Columbia. It has become a private industry in many states, and the entrepreneurs that have taken advantage of these new laws are enjoying record profits. The State of Washington has become the exclusive retail source of marijuana in its state and has earned approximately one billion dollars in that industry. The state reports that the additional revenue has been utilized to address various public works projects and government needs for which there had been little if any revenue. In some form or another, this nation has been in a war on drugs since 1870; and for it, we have little to show. A multibillion annual expenditure in the drug war has not significantly impacted upon the distribution, sale and consumption of illegal drugs. We need a new strategy. History illustrates for us that the prohibition laws of the 1920s were miserably ineffective in the war on alcoholic beverages. And we know how much those laws benefited the criminal element in our nation and adversely affected the quality of life in America. As far as our drug war is concerned, I am confident that it is safe to say it is not working, and I propose the "Trojan Horse" strategy to effectively address this problem and finally win the war. Our government should move to legalize ALL drugs. Yes, each of the substances that are currently illegal to possess in this nation should be legalized. We should follow the model established in the state of Washington and control every aspect of the distribution and sales of these products. I am not suggesting this as surrender. I do not believe that we should allow ourselves to be comfortable with drug use. We should use the revenue generated from the sale of illegal drugs to WIN the war against drugs.

At first glance, there will be some who will argue that legalizing drugs and then having the government sell the drugs will make us drug dealers and no better than the criminals we have been fighting. They will argue that we will create more junkies and thusly become responsible for ruining the lives of millions of people. At present, how difficult is it to purchase illegal drugs ANYWHERE in this country? How often do we learn of instances where the illegal drugs have been cut with substances that enhance the high or kill the purchaser? Controlling all aspects of the drug trade will give us the ability to ensure that no one dies from a tainted product. Most importantly, the revenue generated from this venture will provide the necessary revenue to make available to substance-addicted persons the same quality of care as the Betty Ford Center, Passages of Malibu, et al. At present, lower-income persons do not have access to that level of care, and along with this being a medical issue, it is an economic issue. The drug business is like all other businesses as it is driven by "supply and demand" principles. Winning the war on drugs will require lowering the demand for the product. This cannot be accomplished with disparate treatment opportunities; EVERY person suffering with the illness of addiction MUST have the same treatment opportunities to win this war. The law of "supply and demand" is one of the basic tenets in any study of economics. We cannot continue to ignore the "demand" aspect of our illicit drug problem.

The idea of having our government take over the illicit drug business will be repulsive to some, and that is something that I understand. However, I must advise it is altogether plausible that our government has been clandestinely involved in the illegal drug trade for decades. In 1985, Senator John Kerry initiated a congressional investigation into reports that the CIA was involved in nefarious activities involving the distribution of crack cocaine in major urban cities of

America, Southern California in particular, in order to produce necessary revenue to arm its Contra army in Nicaragua. Senator Kerry's investigation concluded that there was "considerable evidence" to support these allegations. In 1996, Gary Webb wrote a series entitled *Dark Alliance* for the *San Jose Mercury News* which detailed the Iran/Contra operation of the CIA. William Leonard Roberts, better known as the rapper Rick Ross, is identified in Webb's work as one of the major players in this criminal enterprise. It is noteworthy that other journalists have panned Mr. Webb's work; however, there are aspects of his work that coincide with the report Senator Kerry generated eleven years prior.

More recently while trolling the Internet, I was sickened to find images of U.S. Marines providing security for poppy fields in Afghanistan. The same poppy fields that provide considerable revenue (an estimated ONE BILLION DOLLARS) to ISIS and other terror groups—revenue used to purchase weapons used against the U.S. troops. These are the same poppy fields that produce much of the heroin that plagues the streets of America. THIS IS OFFENSIVELY STUPID! When our troops arrived in Afghanistan in 2001 to find Bin Laden and exact a major offensive against the terror groups destroying the poppy fields of Afghanistan should have been at the top of the "to-do" list. An age-old military strategy is to destroy/hinder supply chains for the enemy. The poppy fields of Afghanistan are a major resource for terror organizations around the globe. After landing in Afghanistan, leaflets should have blanketed the poppy fields of Afghanistan to inform the farmers they had three days to vacate the area. They should have been made to understand that unless they loved the smell of napalm in the morning from these fields, you should be gone. I've read that part of the hesitancy to destroy these fields is that the information we receive from the drug lords who own these fields is especially valuable. How valuable is it? Our troops arrived in Afghanistan in 2001, and it wasn't until 2009 that Osama bin Laden was found and killed. And how valuable could any of that information be if the trade-off is to allow the enemy the opportunity to retool AND allow the drug lords the opportunity to continuously poison our nation with their wicked product.

Attorney General Jeff Sessions has stated he will take our drug enforcement effort back to the 1980s…REALLY? The most significant effect the 1980s policies had were to imprison socioeconomically challenged low to mid-level drug dealers to exceptionally long prison terms. These policies had ZERO effect on those who are responsible for the tonnage of drug delivered into our nation. The 1980s policies had ZERO effect upon the billion-dollar drug cartels that dominate South America and Mexico. These policies did not avert the "next-man-up" reality of inner city drug dealing. These policies did not impact upon our urban terrorists, the street gangs. There is nothing in this strategy that considers the financial institutions that may be laundering the illegal drug money. Mr. Sessions I say to you the effectiveness of these policies rank with "Puff the Magic Dragon" or any other fairy tale of which one can think. This requires ZERO imagination and demonstrates a lack of sincere effort. U.S. Marines are safeguarding poppy fields in Afghanistan, and Attorney General Sessions is espousing longer prison sentences for mid-level drug dealers as the answer to our illicit drug problem. In the words of the legendary singer Aretha Franklin, "Who's zoomin' who?"

I propose that we formally and with complete transparency enter the drug business. Clandestinely operating that business to "protect American interests" in other parts of the world and doing such with reckless disregard to the consequences wrought upon AMERICAN cities is EVIL. The hundreds of thousands of lives adversely affected have left an indelible stain on our nation. Only the truly heartless can turn a blind eye to drug-addicted newborns. The clandestinely delivered tonnage of drugs into our inner cities has provided the requisite resources for OUR in-bred terrorists—street gangs. The ever-increasing violence that accompanies the urban terrorists continues to plague our nation. I cannot, will not seek to excuse the criminality of these urban terrorists due to a poor educational system, limited opportunities or even institutional racism. The Lord endowed each of us with "free will," and we CAN do better IF we WANT to do better. Frederick Douglas was born a slave. He lived in a time when had he been caught attempting to read a book; he would have been lynched. But he WANTED more, and he was able to eventually become an adviser to the President of the United States. However, our system CANNOT be excused its part in the development of our street gang epidemic. It is COMPLETELY inexcusable to provide these purveyors of crime and terror with the fuel for their engine of lawlessness.

Opponents to the legalization of drugs will almost certainly point to the yearly number of drug-related deaths experienced in our country. According to the Centers for Disease Control (CDC), there were 166,510 deaths related to methamphetamine over the last ten years. In the same time period 8,257 heroin-related deaths, and last year, there were 38,329 drug overdose deaths (all drugs). In that same ten-year time span, there were more than 4.8 million tobacco-related deaths. Last year, there were 18,146 deaths related to the consumption of alcoholic beverages. In short, overwhelmingly many more people die from the consumption of alcoholic beverages and tobacco than from the use of illicit drugs. There remains a constant effort to inform our citizenry of the perils related to tobacco use and the abuse of alcoholic beverages. We consistently work to inform our children and the population in general about the horror of drug abuse. However, human frailty continues to succumb to the lure of abusing these substances. We must never lose sensitivity to the horrors of drug abuse; however, we must remain mindful that as horrific as drug abuse is many more of our citizenry loses its life to tobacco and alcoholic beverages.

In the 1980s, President Ronald Regan led the "get tough on crime" movement and espoused rhetoric that he would lead the crusade to rid our nation of illegal drugs. His chosen method was to enact legislation that called for mandatory sentencing for persons convicted of possessing crack cocaine. The 1986 Anti-Drug Abuse Act dictated a mandatory five-year sentence for five grams of crack cocaine; however, one had to be in possession of five hundred grams of powdered cocaine for the same sentence. During my career as a Chicago police officer, I arrested a multitude of people for both powdered and crack cocaine. I submitted the substances to the Illinois Police Crime Laboratory for analysis, and in each case, the resultant lab report read: positive for cocaine. The reports did not differentiate crack from powder, COCAINE IS COCAINE. There is no justifiable reason for punishing crack cocaine offenses more harshly than powder cocaine offenses. The obvious objective was to further the socioeconomic divide; perhaps, Mr. Reagan and the presidents who followed him believed socioeconomic status serves as a legitimate enhancement of criminality. In their eyes, perhaps being poor and in most of those cases not well educated makes the criminality more offensive. The only discernable accomplishment of the 1986 Anti-Drug Abuse Act is according to the Sentencing Project Report the 1980 prison count for drug offenders was 40,000. By 2011, that figure ballooned to 500,000. The drug trade continued to flourish. In 2010, the Fair Sentencing Act somewhat leveled the field as it decreased the 100 to 1 weight disparity between crack cocaine and powder cocaine to 18 to 1. However, the state police crime lab reports continue to read the same: positive for cocaine be it crack or powder. I would be remiss if I failed to illustrate that there are people in federal prisons serving more time for crack cocaine offenses than people convicted in state courts for murder. In many instances, a person convicted of second-degree murder in a state court will serve ten of the twenty years to which he was convicted as opposed to a person convicted of a federal drug offense that is serving fifteen, twenty, thirty years, etc., for an offense which did not involve the direct loss of human life.

Winning the war on drugs is the primary objective of my suggestion to formally enter the business of the sales and distribution of drugs. War is costly. Currently, our nation spends approximately forty to fifty billion dollars annually combating a multitrillion-dollar enterprise. We are simply overmatched. Leveling the playing field is essential to our quest for victory. The State of Washington is one of the twenty-nine states that have legalized marijuana possession in some form. Bill I-502 legalized the possession of small quantities of marijuana for persons twenty-one and over. After initial passage of this bill, the State of Washington collected $80 million in tax revenues. At present, the State of Washington projects it shall enjoy one billion dollars in revenue from the marijuana business. In addition to revenue generated, the State of Washington has benefited in revenue not expended. On average, they were spending between $1,000.00 and $2,000.00 for each possession of cannabis arrest. Two hundred million dollars was spent on marijuana enforcement in that state between 2000 and 2010. Bill I-502 has eliminated that expenditure which makes that revenue available for other critical needs of the citizens of that state.

Decriminalization of marijuana has dramatically impacted the criminal court system in the State of Washington. For example, the court entertained 6879 low-level criminal cases in 2011 as opposed to 120 in 2013 after the passage of I-502. The Washington Association of Sheriffs and Police Chiefs reported that between 2012 and 2014, there was a 63% decrease in marijuana law violations. This means the court dockets in that state experienced a noticeable relief: fewer cases which impacts upon all aspects of criminal court efficiency. Let us extrapolate. The Administrative Office of the U.S. Courts reports in 2014 31% of the caseload in federal criminal courts was drug related. In state courts, 33% of those cases were drug related. Legalizing drugs will provide much needed relief for ALL of our criminal courts. State and federal courts will save money; law enforcement agencies will save money as overtime pay for officers who MUST attend court will be reduced. With a reduced caseload, courts will be able to more quickly and efficiently adjudicate matters before them. This will mean that victims and witnesses won't have to wait eighteen to twenty-four months before their cases are heard. Arrestees will not have to languish in county jails for that same period of time awaiting trial. Prosecutors will not be able to use the "wait time" in the county jail as a bargaining tool to extract guilty pleas from indigent arrestees who may be innocent. Judges will not have to consider the overall population of the county jail as a factor when assigning bond. The ripple effect of this action will be decidedly significant.

Taking over the drug industry in this nation will adversely affect organized crime at ALL levels. In light of the fact that the most lucrative venue for the illicit drug industry is the U.S. The South American and Mexican drug cartels will suffer huge financial losses. The major source of income for American street gangs is selling drugs. I recognize that initially, it will take some time to win the confidence of the illegal drug user with regard to making their purchases from a government-operated establishment, but when they recognize they can get a better quality product for LESS money, they will come around. And although we will be providing these "killer" substances, we'll have an opportunity to direct the user to QUALITY programs that will assist them with defeating their addictions. The revenue generated from the sale of these substances will afford EACH drug abuser the opportunity at programs the quality of the Betty Ford Center or Passages at Malibu, to name a few. Quality control over the product can ensure there are no "bad batches" of the product on the street—batches that lead to instances of instant death after use. Our takeover of the industry can have a decided impact upon the violent crime rate; turf wars over who gets to sell where can be eliminated. And though the South American and Mexican drug cartels are heavily armed, I'm confident that a fight with the U.S. military is NOT very appealing.

I am not advocating a change in the policies of any employer regarding the use of intoxicating substances—drugs. IF it is currently company policy that drug users "need not apply" their policies should remain intact without exception. Just as coming to work intoxicated, drunk and smoke-free work environments are "rules of the day" in most places of employment, the employer must remain free to dictate such for that place of employment. Random drug testing is the rule in many government jobs, and our military and forever should that remain. The Controlled Substances Act will require a makeover. Marijuana should never have fallen into the Schedule I category alongside heroin and PCP. The medical community and NOT law enforcement should possess sole dictate regarding this matter.

DUI or DWI, acronyms for driving under the influence or driving while intoxicated, should NOT change. Chemically impaired drivers pose the worse kind of threat, and if anything, the laws enacted to combat these offenses should be stiffened. Standardized Field Sobriety Testing (SFST) has become a basic component of police recruit training nationwide. Additionally, drug recognition expert (DRE) must become a requirement in basic police training. Officers that have affected traffic stops where the officer becomes reasonably suspicious that the driver is chemically impaired should not have to await the arrival of an officer that is certified DRE to proceed with that arrest. In the case of EACH DUI/DWI arrest, the vehicle should be mandatorily impounded; the registered owner should be responsible for the impoundment, towing, and storage fees. Many states hold the registered owner responsible to ensure that a person operating his/her vehicle is in possession of a valid driver's license; and in cases where the driver is not, the owner is subject to penalty. This practice should be nationwide. We must also reign in the discretionary powers of our jurists and ensure laws regarding driver's licenses are STRICTLY enforced. There is NO constitution-ally protected right to drive. The Fifth Amendment protects each of against self-incrimination, and I will NEVER advocate a change in such. However, operating a motor vehicle is an especially responsible exercise. And those who do such MUST be strictly regulated. When a person refuses chemical testing to determine if he/she is impaired, their licenses MUST be suspended MANDATORILY for six months on a first-time occurrence. And for each subsequent offense, the sus-pension should double. A person operating a motor vehicle with a license suspended for refusing to be chemically tested should be MANDATORILY sentenced to jail for six months. On a subsequent offense, that person should be sentenced to a year in prison. Yes, that would make the person a convicted felon…oh darn! Each convic-tion for operating a motor vehicle while impaired should garner a doubling the previous sentence. The safety of the many should far exceed the needs of the few. I recognize the possibility of mitigating circumstances such as medical emergencies and prosecutors should have the flexibility to consider such during the initial phases of the court proceedings. However, the accused with the $500.00 an hour lawyer should NOT have the opportunity to eschew responsibility for his/her criminally negligent behavior.

The potential effect legalizing the possession of marijuana may have upon our youth is a LEGITIMATE concern and most assur-edly not be lost. A study conducted by Washington State Healthy Youth reports there is no significant upswing in the use of cannabis by youngsters. Their study reported usage rates for tenth to twelfth graders slightly decreased. The University of Washington's Alcohol & Drug Abuse Institute has utilized the increased tax revenues to boost its drug education website. As I reflect upon my personal drug education during my youth, I can only wish EACH youngster received the type of education I did. In the seventh grade at Sacred Heart School, Father Thomas Seitz came to our classroom to give us "the talk" on drugs. After Father Seitz finished his instructions on drugs, I was left with the impression that if I smoked a joint, I'd be shooting heroin into my arms three months later. I couldn't wait to get home to tell my parents about the EVILS of drugs. I sat them down and began telling them just how evil drugs were, and that they would never have to be concerned that I would think about using those evil things. After I finished my tutorial, my father stood up and looked down at me. He was a man a few words and had hands the size of baseball mitts. What he said next made me forget EVERYTHING Father Seitz had instructed. My father's message was, "Boy, if you ever use that stuff, I'll be able to look at you and tell it. I brought you here, I'll take you out (this was the most impactful part of his pronouncement), and I'll make another one look just like you." I was twelve years old, and in the mind of this twelve year old, NOTHING about drugs was more important than what my father had just said. In my mind, he could get rid of me and get away with it because there'd be "another one who look just like me." No one would miss me. They wouldn't be able to tell the difference. So from that point on approaching me with a joint or anything like it was an exercise in futility because James Sr. he'd "make another one look just like me." I-502 has provided funding for efforts by the Washington State Liquor Control and Children's Hospital to educational materials for the state's youth. In short, the revenue generated by the sale of marijuana is being used against marijuana.

Chapter 6

GET OFF THE SOFA

"The world will not be destroyed by those who do evil but by those who watch them without doing anything." (Albert Einstein)

In the first four chapters of this book, I have outlined various things that I believe will improve our Criminal Justice System. In the fifth chapter, I offered a source of revenue to pay for said changes while addressing another major challenge that our Criminal Justice faces. In this chapter, I reveal the most important factor for that change: WE THE PEOPLE! "They" will not affect the necessary changes required to make our Criminal Justice System decidedly more effective. WE must affect that change, or it will never become a reality. "We should be the change that we want to see" (John Legend, "If You're Out There"). We must get off the sofa, get involved and assert ourselves as the true, actual, indisputable owners of this republic. Let us beat back the notion of we require paternalist oversight in matters of government: that we are not sophisticated enough to under the intricacies of governance. We cannot push the envelope just far enough to force our elected officials to pass a few "feel good laws" and then retreat to our comfort zone, back to the sofa. "Freedom ain't free"—not a cliché or trendy catch phrase; it is true and irrefutable as 1+1=2. We must remain forever engaged in each and every detail of the operation of our government.

In the five previous chapters, I offered a litany of suggestions that I believe will significantly improve the Criminal Justice System of the United States. Most of what I suggested will command significant capital—a lot of money. I offered a plan to generate the requisite funding for my suggestions, but along with that additional revenue, there will be the temptation to steal. The relentless pursuit of the pagan god money has been the downfall of oh so many people. During our "supposed" war on drugs and our "supposed" war on terror, members of our military have been ordered to protect a product that produces revenue for the "terror" organizations to purchase weapons to use against them. It appears as though this has been commonplace throughout the presidencies of George W. Bush, Barack Obama, and into the presidency of Donald Trump. In centuries past, we have entrusted the purse strings to our elected officials and turned a semiblind eye to what is done with OUR money. In fact, during various periods of time in this nation's history, our elected officials have acted almost with impunity regarding the manner in which our money is spent. In accordance with the U.S. Constitution, the only entity that bears the authority to declare is Congress. Congress last declared war June 4, 1942 against the nations of Romania, Hungary, and Bulgaria; this of course was during World War II. However, our nation has been in fully armed conflict on a multitude of occasions since. It is not my intention to question the necessity of any of those armed conflicts; it is my intention to illustrate to what degree our elected officials will disregard the law (Constitution) when convenient and spend our money in whatever manner they see fit.

The paternalistic attitude of our elected officials is ingrained in this society. It was established in the manner in which our country elects its president. Although the "founding fathers" sought to create a government distinctly different from that from which they came, a hint of aristocracy was established from the beginning. The Electoral College was established because the "founding fathers" did not want to entrust the selection of the president strictly to the "common" folk. The Electoral College was to be the fail-safe, the mechanism in place to protect us from the "tyranny of the majority." Alexander Hamilton states, "The Electoral College is not perfect, it is at least excellent because it ensures that the office of the President will never fall to the lot of any man who is not of eminent degree, endowed with the requisite qualifications." One of the primary concerns was that a candidate from a more populous state would always win the presidency. That the smaller states would have little if any say in the election of the president. In the twenty-first century, that reasoning is as antiquated as the Model T. One of the flaws with the rationale is assuming EACH person in a particular state will vote in lockstep with all other voters in that state. Of course, in the beginning, only white males could vote but is assuming that the vast majority of white men in a particular state are going to vote the same reasonable? In the twenty-first century, the voting population is appreciably more diverse and much more informed. Modern technology affords the voting population many more opportunities for enlightenment: voters have a vast array of information sources. Accordingly, the opinions and viewpoints of the populace are diverse; they cannot be pigeonholed. The condescending viewpoint of the "founding fathers" assisted with establishing the aristocracy which evolved.

I submit the Electoral College is the perfect voter suppression tool. The assumption that the vast majority of voters in any one state will vote the same is preposterous. As evidenced by the fact on five separate occasions the candidate with the most total votes lost the presidential election, this methodology of choosing our president is terrible. The presidential election process has devolved into a contest between "red" states and "blue" states with a few "swing" states in the middle. "United" states would support a process that encourages full voter participation regardless of ideology. If a person resides in a traditionally "blue" state but favors the "red" candidate, he/she is often left with the feeling his/her vote has no value because the majority of the people in the state are going to vote "blue." If the blue candidate becomes president and both houses of Congress are majority "blue," they will spend the next four years beating up on the "red." But if the blue candidate becomes and both houses of Congress are "red," four years of stagnation and a failure to serve the American people will be the result. Oh, but if the "blue" candidate becomes president and one house of Congress is "blue" while the other is "red," a kerfuffle will result.

The Electoral College is an instrument of voter suppression. Individuals living in what may be considered a traditional "blue" state that feel a strong desire to support the "red" candidate in the next election can conclude his/her vote is inconsequential. The all or nothing reality of the Electoral College can dissuade voters, particularly new voters, from participation in the process. One of the greatest strengths of our nation is its diversity. We NEED to hear from all sides, each and every one of our citizens. As I progressed through school, the most valuable thing I came to know is how much I do NOT know. There will never come a time when any one person knows oh so much more than anyone else. We each have our strengths and weaknesses, and we must leave ourselves open to learn from one another.

Our election calendar can also serve as a voter suppression tool. Most elections local or federal are held in the late fall or winter months. In the northern half of the country, weather is ALWAYS a factor regarding movement and/or transportation. If each of our elections, local and federal were to be held in warm weather months, I am confident that voter turnout would be positively impacted. As our nation grows older, the seniors will find it considerably easier to make it to the polling places. In some cases, local incumbents may find heavy voter turnout much more challenging. OH DARN! Heavy voter turnout should make it more difficult for incumbents to be reelected. Incumbents should have their feet held to the fire at each and every turn.

We treat our elected officials more like EMPLOYERS as opposed to EMPLOYEES; far too often, they are treated with a reverence that is inconsistent with the relationship that should exist between the citizenry and its elected officials. We are not the task masters we should be; we fail to consistently place the demands upon our public servants that their jobs command. "No excuses, no explanations," Coach Mike Tomlin states. We must insist that our employees, our elected officials produce real solutions for problems, and that our government become proactive as opposed to reactive. However, consistent with the concept of "respect," if you lack self-respect, you'll never grasp the concept of respect for others. The requisite command over our elected officials will never be attained as long as we are part-time stewards of this republic. This requires full-time and consistent engagement, and this effort must begin NOW!

I have believed in my convictions
And have been convicted for my beliefs
Conned by the Constitution
And harassed by the police…
I've been hoodwinked by professional hoods
My ego has happened to me
It'll be alright, just keep things cool
And take the people off the street
We'll settle all this at the conference table
You just leave everything to me
Which gets me back to my convictions
And being convicted for my beliefs
'Cause I believe these smiles
In three-piece suits
With gracious, liberal demeanor
Took our movement off the streets
And took us to the cleaners
In other words, we let up the pressure
And that was all part of their plan
And every day we allow to slip through our fingers
Is playing right into their hands.

—Gil Scott-Heron, "The New Deal"

Asserting our ownership of our republic is a daunting task which will require multifaceted effort and incredible stamina. The "ruling class" will not cede power easily and shall attempt to use every bit of power at their disposal to preserve the status quo. It is notable that not every elected official is disingenuous in their proc-lamation of service. Three are some terrific elected officials in our nation; however, there are enough disingenuous ones to spoil the pot. Our effort must come together around "ideals & principles" and NOT an individual or individuals. We have to come together, each person seizing a responsibility and fulfilling that responsibility to its conclusion. Inertia is perhaps the most difficult physical property to overcome, and initiating this change will be laborious. However, it is doable, and we owe it to ourselves to make this happen. The "powers that be" are currently nervous about the possible "coming together" of the masses, and in some states, they are attempting preemptive strikes. In Minnesota, lawmakers are considering legislation to bill protestors for the services of police officers during their protests. This hinges upon whether the protest is classified as a public nuisance. (Who gets to make that determination?) Washington State is considering legislation that would make protestors guilty of a Class C felony if they disrupt a business. I wonder if the 1960's lunch counter demonstrators or black people that protested department stores that would not allow them to try on clothing before purchasing or the Montgomery Bus Boycott would qualify as such. lawful assembly and PEACEFUL demonstration are inalienable rights of American citizens. Let us not allow these blatant efforts toward oppression to stand. We must purge every level of government of individuals who seek to repression.

Currently, the U.S. Constitution has established a term limit for the most responsible elected office in this nation: the presidency. The idea behind establishing a term limit for the presidency was to ensure that an individual will not be able to establish an oligarchy or monarchy. I submit the same ideology must be established for EACH elected office in our nation, regardless of what level of government. We must not allow individuals to establish their own personal fiefdoms. Twenty years of service is long enough for the U.S. Senate. A person should be restricted to three elected six-year terms. And yes, this restriction should extend to the judiciary, which should include the U.S. Supreme Court. There should not be a lifetime guarantee of employment for ANY governmental official at ANY level. A consistent infusion of new ideas and energy will better serve our nation than stagnation. We must guard against situations that give an elected official a sense of entitlement. No one in government should be afforded the opportunity to "put a lock" on a particular office. Oftentimes, that leads to situations where the official forgets that he/she is the employee and not the employer. At the federal level, the decade's long debate over health insurance is a sparkling example of how the employees have forgotten for whom they work. I cannot find any situation where the employee enjoys better health insurance than the employer. IF our employees cannot devise a plan to provide each American citizen with the same health insurance plan they enjoy, then they do not deserve a health insurance plan. Ladies and gentlemen, we MUST be this demanding, we MUST insist they place our needs ahead of the special interests groups and campaign financiers. We must establish campaign expenditure limits: elections should not be bought. We must insist upon limits upon how much an individual or a business can donate to any person's campaign. And these limits MUST be ironclad, completely absent of ANY wiggle room. Lobbyists have populated the chambers of government at many levels of government, particularly the federal branch. I propose that effective immediately, there shall be no more lobbyists. Our elected officials should be swayed primarily by the citizens they have been sworn to serve and not a few "big bucks" special interest groups. Many of the major corporations in our country have consistently demonstrated their greed; their drive to earn more money is their ONLY motivation, citizens be damned. We cannot ignore human frailty, so we must remove the temptation of the big campaign contributions. Beloved Illinois Senator Paul Simon stated his decision not to seek reelection was largely influenced by the overwhelming need to fund raise. He decried the fact he had to spend more time fund raising than serving the people of Illinois. We absolutely MUST let it be known that our government is NOT for sale.

Our presidential elections should become nonpartisan; we need a person more committed to serving "we the people" as opposed to a political party. We NEED an American president, not a Democrat, Republican, Libertarian, etc. Let us have a president that first identifies with us as opposed to group of individuals consistently bickering over power. The Executive Branch of government will be better positioned to shepherd the Congress if he/she is independent of a political identity.

We are much more alike than we are different. The current state of our electoral process promotes differences between us. It pits American against American which does not benefit the masses. It does, however, benefit those persons George Carlin identified as the "true owners" of this country. My all-time favorite situation comedy is *All in the Family*. Archie Bunker did a spectacular job of illustrating just how RIDICULOUSLY STUPID bigotry is. I do not believe the biggest social ill this nation suffers is racism. It is my belief that racism is the tool the classicists use to keep the masses of American people bickering and competing over the scraps whilst they sit at the banquet table and feast. Classism was established at the inception of this nation. Alexander Hamilton revealed as much in his defense for the inane concept of the Electoral College. If one looks behind his words, the message of the elitists that founded this nation is that they did not trust the responsibility of selecting the president solely to the masses. We continue to be "hoodwinked by professional hoods." Our most precious commodity, most valuable asset is human life. Each of us is flawed; therefore, not one of us is better than the other. My Christian faith has taught me that the Lord has endowed each of us with "free will." Free will is a wonderful but difficult asset to manage. Most of us manage it fairly well which is why most of us are not criminals. However, there are those of us that have not managed it well, and criminality has been the result. There is no utopia; there will NEVER be a perfect society. However, we would be remiss if we ceased to work diligently toward achieving perfection. Regardless of one's religious faith or lack thereof, common decency dictates that we WORK toward making our society the best it can be. The basic essentials of life—food, clothing, housing, health care, education, safety—should not be impacted by the socioeconomic status of the individual. Coming together to live in a communal society should ensure that EACH of the members of that society has equal access to the amenities that society offers; IF they WORK to achieve such. There should be no barriers, overt or covert to realizing those goals. Tragically, over the years, we've become a nation of excuses as "the owners" have fostered such. Ducking responsibility contributes mightily to the turmoil in which we live. If we fail to hold ourselves accountable, fail to meet our own responsibilities, we can in no way hold accountable those with whom the operation of our government is their duty. "The owners" benefit greatly from a public with limited vision and ambition. Our retail-driven economy can work to enslave us as we have allowed materialism to define our sense of self-worth. Let us pull back the curtain and expose the wizard. I will be accused of oversimplifying some or many things. One of my goals has been to expose the needless obfuscation of certain aspects of our society and to illustrate that only those at the top of the food chain have benefited. Overcoming the inertia to accomplish the necessary change in our Criminal Justice System will take herculean effort, and it will not happen quickly. But it will not begin until we get off the sofa, put our hard hats on and get to work.

Thank you for your attention.

JB

ABOUT THE AUTHOR

James B. Bolen was born and raised on the south side of Chicago in the Englewood community. He was fortunate enough to attend twelve years of Catholic School before enlisting in the United States Marine Corps. After being honorably discharged from the Marine Corps, Bolen returned home to Chicago where he studied Criminal Justice at the University of Illinois at Chicago. James Bolen joined the Chicago Police Department in January 1992. During his fifteen-year career, he received four department commendations and twenty-one honorable mentions. He spent the bulk of his policing career working in the Englewood community in which he grew up.